Gabe's tongue refused to form any words as he stared at the woman across from him. This wasn't catching up, and discussing Maine's snow versus Texas's heat shouldn't make him want to kiss her. Shouldn't make him want to run his hand along her waist… Shouldn't make him want so many things.

"I missed you when you left the theater. After we…" Her cheeks bloomed as she tilted her wineglass back. "You were my first kiss."

The words were so soft that Gabe wondered if Tessa had meant to say them out loud. "You were mine, too. I even went to the Trinity versus Bell football game senior year, hoping you'd be there. I wanted to apologize for vanishing. To explain that the job I got paid better and started immediately. To ask for your number." Gabe grinned. "If only every teen had had a cell then."

"If only…" Tessa took another sip of her wine, then set it on the table.

"If only…" Gabe repeated.

Dear Reader,

For my fourth medical romance, I went home. Or as close to home as I could get! I grew up in one of the many suburbs around Dallas, Texas. Yes, even after living in Ohio for over fifteen years, I still have a Texan drawl. I am married to an Ohioan and my girls are snow lovers, but I will always be a Texas girl at heart. So it was fun to head home for this story.

Dr. Tessa Garcia's been burned by love. She gave up a promotion because her ex-husband didn't want to move, and she's determined not to give up another one. But when a passionate night with Gabe results in twins, can she find a way to have it all?

Pediatric nurse Gabe Davis is a helper, a protector. After losing his fiancée, he's come home to Texas for a fresh start. He may not have planned to start a family with Tessa, but as they grow closer, there is no place he'd rather be. But what if the woman he loves doesn't want or need his help? Can he convince his independent love that he wants more than just their twins—he needs her heart?

Juliette Hyland

THE PEDIATRICIAN'S TWIN BOMBSHELL

JULIETTE HYLAND

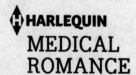

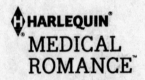

HARLEQUIN®
MEDICAL
ROMANCE™

Recycling programs
for this product may
not exist in your area.

ISBN-13: 978-1-335-40457-2

The Pediatrician's Twin Bombshell

Juliette Hyland began crafting heroes and heroines in high school. She lives in Ohio with her Prince Charming, who has patiently listened to many rants regarding characters failing to follow the outline. When not working on fun and flirty happily-ever-afters, Juliette can be found spending time with her beautiful daughters, giant dogs or sewing uneven stitches with her sewing machine.

Books by Juliette Hyland

Harlequin Medical Romance

Unlocking the Ex-Army Doc's Heart
Falling Again for the Single Dad
A Stolen Kiss with the Midwife

Visit the Author Profile page at Harlequin.com.

For Dot. You're missed beyond measure.

CHAPTER ONE

Dr. Tessa Garcia leaned against the bar and slid the back of her heel out of the four-inch peep-toe shoes she'd crammed her feet into. The shoes had been uncomfortable when she'd purchased them three years ago, but she didn't remember them being such torture devices.

What had possessed her to wear them?

The same ridiculous urge that had driven her to give in to Lily's plea that she come tonight. Tessa had hoped that this outing might stem the loneliness that clawed at her when she collapsed into bed. At least for an hour.

She should have known better. But she'd wanted to believe she might still have a place with these people.

That she wasn't completely alone.

Tessa glared at the martini sign hanging from the bar. The former dive bar had been revamped over the last year. The pathetic-looking burned-out neon bar signs were now upscale artwork.

But the worn bar and exposed brick walls were still the same. Likely a design aesthetic Tessa didn't understand—or maybe the new owners had run out of money during their revitalization effort.

Revitalization. Tessa hated that word. Out with the old, in with the new—the phrase applied to people, too, apparently.

A cackle went up from the patio, and Tessa hated the heat coating her cheeks. She didn't belong here now. This had always been Max's place. His social circle, his night to shine. She'd been a girlfriend, and then a wife, but never a friend. That realization sent more regret washing through her.

They'd divorced a little over a year ago, though they'd inhabited the realm of uncomfortable roommates instead of spouses for far too long. She and Max might not have been able to save their union, but she hadn't thought the women she'd considered friends would also be casualties of their failed marriage.

But they were all married to Max's college buddies. God, Tessa wanted to slap herself. She should have been smart enough to make that connection.

Maybe if she had spoken to anyone outside the hospital in the last month besides food delivery people...

Tessa's eyes looked to the ceiling as her foolishness washed over her—again. The people in the corner had all stared when she'd popped in, the press of pity in their gazes as they tried to pretend it was fine that she'd stopped by. Even Lily's bright exclamations hadn't been able to cover the pink on her cheeks as her eyes darted between Tessa and her ex-husband's new bride.

Her divorce had been easy—at least on paper. Her lawyer had called it textbook. She and Max had divided their savings account, sold the starter home they'd purchased and said goodbye to their shared lives. It was the *after* that had rocked her.

In all her failed attempts to make him happy, Max's hobbies and dreams had taken precedent. When she'd suggested hiking or visiting the botanical gardens, or even hanging out in the backyard where she'd cultivated a relaxing green space, he'd balked. He'd point out that she was always asking him to do more than his share of things. That she should want to do what he wanted, since he was handling everything at home so she could advance at the hospital.

That hadn't been the full truth. He'd done slightly more than half the chores and complained every step of the way. But she'd given in every time. That still rankled.

Her father hadn't appreciated being asked to do anything for his family, either. Tessa's mom had always made excuses for him—just like Tessa had for Max. Tessa had watched her mom try everything to hold on to her marriage. Then she'd watched the catastrophic aftermath.

She'd witnessed all of it, and rather than protecting herself, Tessa had given in to a man's desires, too, hoping that by ceding her likes, her friends, *her dreams*, Max might look at her like he had when they first started dating, hoping that she could have the happy family she'd always craved.

As an only child, Tessa had longed for siblings. For a home life that didn't rock between stony silence and angry shouts. Tessa had wanted to believe her union would differ from her mother's. But life rarely produced fairy tales, and the Garcia women always seemed to end up alone.

At least she had a thriving career as a pediatric attending at Dallas Children's Hospital. Her ex-husband hadn't been able to strip that from her, though he had stolen the promotion they had offered her at Cincinnati Children's.

Maybe Tessa should have moved without him. But she hadn't been willing to admit what, deep down, she'd already known. Her marriage had been over long before they'd finalized the divorce decree.

She'd put so much of herself aside for Max, and what did she have? A closet full of colorful scrubs—and comfy shoes. And no one to grab drinks with. No one to see a movie or go to the botanical garden with. No one at the other end of the phone. *And no senior attending position.*

Hell, she'd even given up the garden she'd cultivated so carefully because Max had wanted to sell their home. Instead of fighting or making a sound argument for why she should purchase it, Tessa had just consented to the sale.

Her townhome didn't have a lot of extra space for a garden. Tessa harrumphed as she spun the ice around her cup. She'd been so focused on finding a spot close to work—and away from her ex—that she'd rushed the purchase. But she had her independence, and she would never let a man dictate her path again.

"I didn't think Max and Stephanie were coming." Lily's cheeks were red as she fanned herself and waved for another drink. "I swear, she's barely old enough to be in here." Lily dramatically rolled her eyes to the ceiling as she leaned against the bar.

"Mmm-hmm." Tessa kept her gaze focused on the ice melting in the glass that once held club soda. Lily might not be drunk…yet, but the wife of her ex-husband's oldest friend was tipsy enough to repeat anything Tessa might say.

At least the bubbly blonde had interrupted Tessa's pity party.

"It was nice to see you. Guess I probably shouldn't—"

She bit back the last part of that sentence, but Tessa had no problems filling in the silence. This would be the last time she was invited.

A martini appeared in front of them, and Lily sighed. "If I hear one more word about college sports…" Her first sip almost emptied the fancy glass. She laid her hand on Tessa's arm and then flounced back to the patio.

College athletics might not be interesting, but, apparently, neither was spending time with an ex-wife who didn't know her place. Lily clearly regretted the multiple texts she'd sent begging Tessa to show up tonight.

Not that it really mattered.

Over the years, girlfriends had come and gone, and now she was the first wife who was being booted from the group. It was past time for her to go home.

"Those heels look like hell."

She sighed. Flirting in a bar had never been her scene, but flirting in a bar where her ex-husband and all his friends were drinking felt like an extra level of desperation.

And she was not desperate. Lonely, but not desperate. *Never desperate.*

"I've already asked for the check and am going home to get out of these torture devi—" Her tongue froze as she met the honey eyes next to her.

God, he was gorgeous! His dark hair was trimmed, but a bit of a five o'clock shadow accented his firm jaw. His arms were muscular without looking like all he did was grunt in front of a gym mirror and drop weights on the floor.

Clearing her throat, she held up her empty glass and tried to push the unexpected arousal away. The man before her was extraordinary.

"Just let me strike out. Then I can tell my sister I tried and go home myself." He winked before waving over her shoulder. "If you want to throw the ice in my face to make it look really convincing, she will definitely let me off the hook."

Tessa laughed and had to stop herself from leaning closer. "I've never thrown anything in someone's face. But now I kind of want to."

"The option stands." Two dimples appeared in the Adonis's cheeks. "But if you keep laughing, it won't be believable—though I wouldn't complain. Even with the air-conditioning, this place still feels like an outer ring of—"

He caught the last word, and Tessa beamed. "Not from Texas, then?" The question slipped between them, and she gripped her glass. She hadn't meant to drag out this encounter, but she suddenly didn't want it to end.

She really needed to make some new friends…

or set up a dating profile on one of the apps the single medical professionals were always discussing. *No.* She was not interested in that.

But what was five extra minutes in this hellhole, if it was with the dreamboat before her? At least he'd give her something delicious to think about in her lonely bed tonight.

"Originally, yes. But I've been out of the state for years. I forgot how hot it was in Dallas in June." He leaned over her shoulder, then shook his head. "She just gave me a thumbs-up. Ah, well, I can still tell her you told me to take a hike in a few minutes. I'm Gabe."

"Gabe?" The subtle shift in his voice tickled the back of her brain. Her gaze wandered his chiseled cheeks, and the bite of recognition stole through her. *It couldn't be...* "Gabe Davis?"

Tessa blinked as she tried to reconcile the stunning hunk before her with the teenager who'd spent a summer working with her in the Tinseltown theater. The honey eyes and smile were the same, and her mood lightened even further as he tilted his head and raised an eyebrow. He'd been cute then, and most of the staff had swooned over him.

Tessa had, too. They'd even shared an impromptu kiss late one night.

Then he'd disappeared.

She gave her best fake smile, "You forgot to

tell me you'd like extra butter layered in your popcorn. *Of course* it's not too much trouble to get you a fresh one."

"Tessa Garcia!"

Gabe's deep chuckle rumbled through her, and this time Tessa didn't stop herself as she leaned closer. "I'd heard you left Texas. I assume it was for someplace cooler, given your hatred of this lovely June evening."

She bit the inside of her cheek as that piece of information floated out. She hadn't gone looking for him…not really. He'd been a recommended friend on social media, and she'd clicked on his profile once. Just for nostalgia's sake.

There'd been a picture of a lot of snow and a notice that he only shared his information with friends. She'd almost pushed the bright blue request button, but she'd resisted. Barely.

"I was in Maine. Just moved back." A shadow passed over Gabe's eyes as he signaled for the bartender, but it disappeared quickly.

If she'd had something other than club soda in her glass, she might be able to pretend the haunted gaze had never existed. But she was at a bar avoiding her ex-husband and his friends, so who was she to pass any judgment?

"Can I get a Coke and—" he turned to Tessa "—I owe you a drink for saving me from my sister's matchmaking schemes."

"Club soda with lime." Tessa pursed her lips as the barkeep barely kept the smile on his face. She'd worked in a bar through college and knew their tab wasn't enough to keep the great service coming. Still, she laid some extra on the counter as he put the two cups in front of them. "To cover the first club soda."

The man's shoulders relaxed a little, and he added an extra lime before passing them the drinks.

"If you're up for it, why don't we see if there are any seats on the patio? Get you off those dastardly high heels."

"My ex-husband is back there with his new wife." The words slipped from her lips, and Tessa could have throttled herself. The last person she wanted to talk about was her ex. But she also didn't want to sit back there talking to Gabe while all the people she'd thought were her friends either ignored her or studied this interaction.

"I really was getting ready to leave when you walked up. It wasn't a lie." She raised the drink to her lips, enjoying the bubbles tickling her nose. "Pathetic, I know."

"Nope." Gabe shook his head. "Plus, this saves me having to politely pretend I'm not sweltering back there while we nurse our nonalcoholic beverages and try to figure out how long we have to play catch-up."

He tilted his glass toward her, and his dimples sent another rush down her back. Pressing her fingers to her lips, she shook her head. How did this man make her swoon with just a few minutes of conversation?

"What if I want to catch up?" The question surprised her, but it was the sincerity behind it that nearly made her knees buckle. She wanted to catch up with Gabe. Wanted to know what the gorgeous, clever man—whose sister was thrilled he was talking to someone in a bar—had done for the last two decades.

Maybe discover why he'd disappeared after they'd kissed. *No.* That was not a question she was going to ask.

They'd had fun working behind the concession stand at the theater and goofed off more than they probably should when the theater was dead on the weeknights. But they hadn't gone to the same high school. Their final flirtation, which had led to her first kiss, had felt like…well, it had felt like the rush of first crushes that only teenagers could experience.

She still remembered being hurt that he hadn't warned her he was quitting. If it had been a few years later, cell phones and social media could have transitioned their flirtation into a more genuine connection. But those things had still been just over the horizon.

"I wouldn't mind playing catch-up. Do you want to down that drink, and we can head to another place? Someplace where your ex isn't around?" The ridges of his cheeks darkened as he made the offer.

Was he as out of practice at this as she was? Tessa doubted anyone could be as rusty in the dating field as her. She and Max had met in their freshman dorm and dated all through college. They'd married just before she started med school, and he'd gone to work in finance. She'd been off the market for most of her adult life.

"My place is just around the corner. I have wine and a patio that overlooks the community pond." Heat engulfed her body as she met those sultry eyes again. "I… I… I just meant that it's a good place for me to dump these shoes. And then you can come back to your sister after a drink on my patio."

Nope… There was definitely no one rustier than her at this. And she wasn't even trying to flirt. Well, maybe a little, but not like "invite a stranger back to your condo fifteen minutes after he buys you a club soda."

He took a sip of his drink, and her breath caught as she watched him mull the offer over. If he said no, it would be fine. Better than fine—

it would be the right answer. But Tessa didn't want Gabe to say no. She wanted him to want her—at least for a night of friendly conversation on a condo porch.

How long had it been since someone outside the hospital wanted to spend time with her? Tessa didn't want to calculate that answer.

"Sure," Gabe finally stated. He looked over her shoulder again and smiled. "But just so you know, I'm telling my sister this went perfectly and counting it as a date. That will get her off my back for at least the next three days. Maybe even an entire week!"

Laughter again bubbled in Tessa's chest. How had he taken the most awkward moment ever and made it seem like she was helping him? And how was this gorgeous man still single?

He grinned, dimples deep in each cheek before heading to speak to his sister.

Another round of laughs echoed from the back corner, but most of its sting had evaporated. She laid another couple of dollars on the bar and spared one more glance at the over-the-top decor, then let her mind wander to Gabe's delicious dimples. She could get lost in that smile.

Maybe for more than one night.

That thought sent a cold bead of sweat down her back. She was not interested in dating anyone—even if she was more than a little tired of curling up with a pillow each night.

The position for senior emergency room attending was opening in a few weeks. Assuming the rumors were true.

And she'd learned the hard way that men did not appreciate a successful woman. Oh, they claimed to. Max had said he loved Tessa's drive for success. Asserted that her being so successful made them a power couple—a term Tessa hated.

Then his finance career had stagnated following several poor business decisions and the recession. When he was laid off, Max had grown increasingly agitated by his lack of job prospects. She'd understood, but after he accepted another position, their relationship had still raced toward its explosive end.

Particularly when she'd been offered the senior attending job at Cincinnati Children's. He'd refused to even consider moving for her job and suggested that it would be too much of a commitment if she wanted to start a family anytime soon.

So she'd stayed. Given up the promotion hoping that her sacrifice could repair the divide that had widened between her and her ex. Instead, he'd filed for divorce, claiming Tessa didn't need him for anything besides housework.

It had been a BS excuse—particularly considering he'd married again before the ink had dried on their divorce decree. But it was proof that many men couldn't handle being equal partners in a relationship. They always wanted to be more than their partner. And Tessa didn't have the time to wade through the dating landscape to figure out the good from the bad.

She licked her lips as she subtly checked out Gabe's beautiful derriere. If her heart thumped a bit as Gabe leaned over to tell his sister he was going to Tessa's place for a short while, that was just a symptom of loneliness and nostalgia for an old crush. A one-night escape.

Nothing more.

"I won't wait. You can just order an Uber." Isla's grin was too wide, but Gabe didn't want to disappoint his sister with the truth. He and Tessa were just catching up...which didn't explain the heat running through him, or his willingness to go back to her place.

She was uncomfortable at the bar. Her tanned skin had reddened after she'd invited him to have a drink on her patio, her gaze refusing to meet his. If any other person had made what sounded like such a bold request, he'd have found a polite way to demure. To redirect the conversation to something humorous, something that didn't sound like a direct refusal.

Gabe had only approached Tessa at the bar because he'd assumed the walled-off brunette would shut him down. She'd barely acknowledged the three men he'd watched confidently stride over to her. She'd raised her near-empty glass and waved them away.

He'd watched her lift her feet out of those absurd spikes and been certain she was about to call it a night. And the clock hadn't even struck eight. She'd been perfect.

All he'd needed was a refusal. Then he could pretend to be off his game for the rest of the night. That part would have been the truth.

Gabe Davis had been off his game for the last six years. If life had gone according to plan, he'd have been celebrating his fifth wedding anniversary to Olive this year. Maybe even have a toddler or two to keep their life busy.

But life hadn't followed the plan—it had shredded it. Something Gabe should have been used to. He'd learned at sixteen that the movie version of family and love was a fantasy.

A sitcom reality that drove advertisers to Saturday-morning cartoons and after-school specials. That laid the groundwork for kids to believe in happily-ever-after, leaving them vulnerable to the heartbreak that life seemed all too willing to deliver.

But instead of rejection at the bar, he'd found

Tessa Garcia, the girl who could make a slow shift fly by in giggles and fun. Tessa had been a bright ray of sun at a dark time.

He'd applied for a job at the theater two weeks after his mother announced over pot roast that she'd finished her family experiment.

His mother had loved her career and the accolades that came as she climbed the corporate ladder more than she'd loved her children, and significantly more than she'd loved the man she'd married. But it was the word *experiment* that time hadn't driven from his mind. That still sent fury through him.

He'd shadowed his mom, always praying that he'd earn a bit of her praise. Of her love. Trying to earn things that other mothers gave so freely to their children. But his acts of service had earned him nothing when she'd packed her bags.

He should have quit almost as soon as he started. The theater had sent him home far too often on slow nights, and Gabe needed the money to help his dad. But he'd stayed because working with Tessa had made him happy. For a few hours he could forget the turmoil of his life at home.

He could still remember finally working up the courage to kiss her after they'd closed one night. It had been the highlight of his high school experience.

But the veterinary clinic had called the next day to offer him the afternoon and weekend front desk assistant position, starting immediately. He hadn't been able to turn that down.

His father had already been working two jobs and asking him to drive Gabe to the theater had seemed selfish, particularly when he didn't know her schedule. By the time he'd finally earned enough to buy a rusted-out car that barely ran, she'd left the theater, too.

He'd gone to the football game when her school played his—the only one he'd ever made it to—but if Tessa had been in the crowd, Gabe hadn't been able to find her. He'd left feeling defeated.

When she'd recognized him tonight, his lonely heart had lit up. The freckles on her cheeks had lifted as her lips turned up. The pretty young teenager had turned into a stunning woman. And a night of catching up was all his heart craved.

"Have fun." Isla's laughter was bright, but Gabe didn't turn around.

He could spend as much time as he wanted with his sister. Reconnecting with Tessa at a bar felt...well, he didn't know how to explain the emotions darting through him.

After the offer had spilled from her lips, Gabe had watched Tessa's eyes dart to the corner. He'd waited a moment, expecting her to withdraw the offer, disquieted by the twinge of longing rushing through him. When she hadn't, Gabe's heart had sped up—just a tick. He hadn't felt that brush of anticipation in so long.

He didn't want to let it go—at least not yet. "Ready?"

"To get out of these?" She gestured to her feet, where red spots were forming on the edges of her big toe, and the back of her heel had to be rubbed raw. "Absolutely!"

"Are you going to make it?"

Tessa sent one more glare south and then shrugged. "No other choice."

For a second Gabe considered offering her a piggyback ride. It was something they'd done more than a few times on slow nights at the theater, racing down the halls, keeping their laughs as quiet as possible for the dozen people seeing movies on a random Tuesday.

He'd enjoyed every moment of her pressed against him. The thrill of her cheek against his as they passed life-size movie cutouts.

Such an offer would be absurd now. They were adults, not goofy teens in the throes of first crushes. No matter how much the urge to help her pulsed through him.

That was just his nature. Gabe was a helper—all his siblings teased him about trying to do everything for everyone. Stacy often reminded him that he didn't have to do everything, but he enjoyed it. Gabe needed to be needed. And it had been so long since anyone had needed him.

It was just that side of him calling to Tessa, wanting to offer an old friend some comfort. If his heart yearned to see if her laughter still sounded the same or if her cheek pressed against his could bring joy back to his life, well, that was just a symptom of nostalgia. He didn't believe the lie his brain was feeding him, but it didn't matter. He would not do anything to break the evening's spell.

The walk to her condo lasted less than ten minutes, and he let out a breath as she stopped in front of the Boardwalk Complex. The most expensive condos in the Dallas area. The developer had bragged in more than one interview that he'd always dreamed of making a property worthy of the most expensive spot in the Monopoly game. It was exactly the type of place his mother would love.

What does Tessa do for a living to live here? He braced himself for opulence as he stepped through Tessa's heavy front door.

But the entry was bright and airy—nothing like his mother's upscale unit where she'd fretted over her breakable finery the few times he and his siblings had visited. A stack of gardening books was piled next to the gray couch, and a bright yellow blanket popped with color. The condo had a light floral scent that sent a thrill through Gabe. The home felt like home.

Which was impossible—and unsettling.

When was the last time he'd felt like anywhere was home? In the months before Olive's passing. Their apartment could have mostly fit in Tessa's spacious living room, but it had been a happy place.

Another wave of nostalgia rushed through him as Tessa grinned and pulled him toward her kitchen. The pinch of longing he hadn't felt in forever bloomed in his chest—again. He was lonelier than he'd realized.

"I have Diet Coke, water and wine." Tessa's voice was soft as her dark eyes held his.

What was he doing here? Gabe had never gone back to a woman's place right after meeting her. Except he knew Tessa, sort of…

But was the memory of teenage Tessa the only reason he was here?

Gabe didn't wish to investigate that question. Clearing his throat, he tried to ignore the flutters in his stomach. "Wine sounds great, but get out of those heels first. Point me in the direction of the bottle opener and glasses. Might as well let me earn my keep." Gabe's fingers brushed hers as she handed him the chilled bottle. Her warmth ran up her fingers to his. Such a minor touch that was over too soon.

Get it together. The innocent touch was nothing—really. This was a friendly catch-up session. A way for two lonely people to feel less alone for a few hours.

"Thank you." Tessa raised out of the heels as she pointed to a cabinet. "But these monstrosities—" she glared at the heels as she lifted them up "—are going directly in the trash! No woman should be subjected to such pain."

Gabe chuckled as he pulled two glasses down. "I think my sister Isla may have just shuddered." At Tessa's confused look, Gabe continued, "She's a buyer for a very fancy department store. She worked for years to become their main shoe buyer."

"Well, you are free to tell her that these are evil!" Tessa's laugh was deeper now, but it still had the lilting edge at the end he'd craved so long ago. The part of Gabe that had been mostly silent since Olive's departure burst open.

Handing her a wineglass, Gabe tipped his own up, trying to ignore the dangerous combination of ancient feelings and new desires. "To old friends and comfortable shoes."

Her dark eyes shimmered as she met his gaze and raised her glass to her lips. "The patio is this way." Her hand gripped his and her gaze floated across him again before she dropped it.

Did her palm tingle, too? The connection had been too brief and too long all at once.

"So, what brought you back to Dallas? Too much snow?" Tessa crossed her legs as she sat on the wicker love seat on her patio.

Gabe slipped in next to her, aware of how close the beauty by his side was. His neck burned. And he couldn't pretend it was the heat of the evening, particularly with the bright umbrella covering them with shade while the sun set. Her soft scent mixed with the evening breeze, calling to him. The intimacy of the setting was thrilling.

And terrifying.

Maine had been Olive's home. And he'd happily returned with her after they'd graduated from nursing school. But it hadn't felt like home with her gone. And after so many years, he'd finally felt ready to leave. The yearning to return to his home, to find a new life—whatever that meant now—had finally sent him back to the Texas heat. Swallowing the cascade of emotions floating through him, Gabe knew there was no way to articulate all those thoughts.

"The snow is not that bad." Gabe didn't directly answer her question, but the response was safer.

At least he thought it was, until Tessa playfully shivered and drew a millimeter closer to him. Her full lips were tinged with red wine, and the urge to dip his head to hers made it hard to breathe. Gabe lifted his glass, never taking his eyes from Tessa. "What is it with Texans and hating snow?"

"It's cold." Tessa held up a finger as she continued to tick off her reasons. "It's slushy. It makes driving difficult. It's cold."

"You already said that one."

"It bears repeating!"

Tessa's hand tapped his knee, and Gabe pinched his wineglass to keep from laying his hand over hers. What was wrong with him? He yearned to make her laugh, to see the hint of a dimple when her lips tipped up. To pull her close.

A small voice in the back of his brain wondered if he should take his leave—chalk the evening up to nostalgia and move on. But it was easy to ignore when Tessa smiled.

He leaned closer. "What Texans don't understand is that snowy weather just means you have to cuddle closer." The flirtation escaped his lips. Gabe watched an emotion he wanted to believe was desire flash in Tessa's eyes.

"I guess that could be true." Her tongue ran along the edge of her lip as she closed a bit more of the distance between them. "But the heat can be—" her gaze darted behind him before she pulled back "—sensual, too."

True… Gabe's tongue refused to form any more words as he stared at the woman across from him. This wasn't catching up, and discussing Maine's snow versus Texas's heat shouldn't make him want to kiss her. Shouldn't make him want to run his hand along her waist…shouldn't make him want so many things.

"I missed you when you left the theater. After we…" Her cheeks bloomed as she tilted her wineglass back. "You were my first kiss."

The words were so soft that Gabe wondered if Tessa had meant to say them out loud. "You were mine, too. I even went to the Trinity versus Bell football game senior year, hoping you'd be there. I wanted to apologize for vanishing. To explain that the job I got paid better and started immediately. To ask for your number." Gabe grinned. "If only every teen had had a cell then."

"If only…" Tessa took another sip of her wine, then set it on the table.

"If only…" Gabe repeated, setting his wineglass next to hers. Without the glass in his fingers, his palms itched to reach out to Tessa. The urge to follow a path that might lead somewhere ignited in him. Gabe crossed his arms, trying to redirect the desire.

It didn't work.

"So now, on to the major questions." Tessa's smile was infectious as she shifted beside him. "Why is your sister trying to set you up at a bar?" Her nose twitched. "You were cute when we worked together, but…" She gestured toward him. "I can't imagine you having trouble getting a date."

No. Gabe hadn't had any trouble getting a date, or he likely wouldn't have, if he'd had any interest in the dating scene. But his heart had gone dark after he'd lost Olive. An empty shell had occupied his chest for years. When it had finally started beating again, Gabe hadn't known what to do. But getting involved with someone new had held little appeal.

So what was he doing here?

"I was with someone for a long time." Gabe's heart hammered, but the sting of loss was muted now. Grief never vanished, but you learned to move around it. And with time, the memories, like Olive's bright laugh and her good heart, came easier. She would have loved Tessa's commentary on high heels. "She passed away."

Warm hands found his, and the cavity in his chest lit up again. Tessa's presence called to him in a way he'd never expected to feel again. His thumb rubbed along the edge of her wrist, just enjoying the connection.

"I'm so sorry, Gabe."

"Thanks. It's been over six years. The pain is distant now, but Isla wants to see me happy again. Of course, her idea of happy is me giving her more nieces and nephews to idolize. I guess Stacy's and Matt's kids aren't enough to sate the great Aunt Isla."

"You're an uncle!" Tessa squeezed his hand again.

Tessa's pressure was light, but it grounded him in a way that Gabe hadn't felt for years. *Six years.* The sensation was comforting—one more surprising element to add to tonight's growing list.

"Yes. My brother Matt has two young boys, and Stacy has two preteen girls and a three-year-old daughter who drives them all batty." Being nearby to help his siblings with their growing broods had been part of Texas's siren call, though Gabe wasn't needed for much.

"That's lovely," Tessa sighed.

"When you are goaded to approach a stranger in a bar, it doesn't feel that way. Though tonight worked out better than I could have hoped." That was the truth. Isla had probably texted everyone the moment he left. How would they feel when he told them that this was just catching up with an old friend?

Except it felt deeper.

That was a dangerous thought. And one that

Gabe didn't wish to examine too closely. Everything had seemed easy from the moment he'd stepped up to Tessa at the bar. If he tried to unravel the mix of thoughts and emotions, it might get messy. At least for tonight, he just wanted to enjoy Tessa's company—for as long as she wanted him here.

"I meant the family meddling." Tessa sighed. "I'm an only child. I haven't seen my father since I was seven, and my mother passed when I was thirteen. They were both only children, too, so no cousins to speak of. I used to daydream about having a huge family." She grinned. "About sisters I could tell secrets to. Or a few brothers who might want to protect me."

Protect me. He felt his lips dip. Everyone should have someone to look out for them. Someone to run to when the world tilted unexpectedly.

"Children's imaginations are something, huh." Tessa rubbed her fingers on her lips and looked over his shoulder before meeting his gaze.

"I'm sure the Davis clan would adopt you." The offer hovered between them as Gabe smoothed his thumb along her wrist, again. The connection electrified him, and Gabe couldn't have dropped it even if he'd wanted to.

It wasn't an errant statement, either. He was sure that Stacy and Isla would willingly welcome the woman before him into their friendship group. If his sisters adopted Tessa, he'd get to see her often, too. That held so much appeal— and sent a thread of worry dancing through him.

Tonight felt like the perfect spell. But perfection was an illusion. If he fell for Tessa and lost on the gamble... His heart constricted just at the thought. He wasn't sure it could survive another battering.

But he didn't withdraw the offer.

"The heat of the day is finally breaking." Tessa didn't address his suggestion, but she didn't let go of his hand, either.

"And at ten o'clock!" Gabe chuckled. *Somehow they were back to the weather.*

Tessa picked up her half-full wineglass and stared at the lukewarm contents. "Maybe we should have opted for the soda." She let go of his hand and uncurled her feet.

Gabe opened and closed his palm, trying to chase the sensation of emptiness away. The night was ending, as it should, but Gabe desperately wanted to pause time. To sit here with Tessa for hours, watch the sunrise and just be with her.

As she stood, her feet wobbled, and Gabe reached for her. She landed in his lap, her mouth falling open as she stared at him. "My feet fell asleep."

Gabe pushed a tight curl behind her ear. *God, she is gorgeous.* "It's okay."

Heat that had nothing to do with the Texas night crackled between them. When her lips met his, Gabe's body released tension he hadn't even realized he'd been holding. Tessa's fingers were heavy on his chest as she deepened the kiss.

The taste of wine lingered on her lips. This wasn't the innocent young kiss they'd shared as teens. This was deeper, electric, and the longing buried within it drove him close to the edge.

Tessa... All his senses lit with longing. *Tessa.*

She pulled back, and Gabe had to reach for all his control not to pull her close again.

"Do you want to go inside?" Tessa bit her lip as her fingers danced across his chest, each stroke sending another jolt through him.

"Yes." There was nowhere else he wanted to be tonight.

CHAPTER TWO

GABE'S WARMTH CARRIED through her as Tessa led them up the stairs. Her breath caught as she saw her bedroom door. She wanted Gabe, he wanted her, and they were single. She needed to lose herself, feel desired, cared for.

At least for one night.

His lips grazed the back of her neck, and the final flutters of nervousness floated away. Turning in his arms, Tessa locked her hands behind his neck and kissed him. His arms tightened around her as his mouth captured hers.

This wasn't a flirtatious test kiss. This was demanding and needy. It was everything, and her body reacted in ways she hadn't experienced in years—maybe ever. Her fingers caressed his back, loving the feel of his body as he molded against her.

They fit perfectly.

It was a ridiculous thought, but it sent shock waves through her as his fingers ran along her sides, each stroke growing bolder before he finally traced his thumb across her nipple. Even through her top, his touch burned. His lips trailed along her neck, and Tessa thought she might explode just from the heat of his lips. "Gabe…"

His name on her lips brought his honey gaze to hers. "Tessa." He dropped a soft kiss along the edge of her jaw. "Do you want to stop?"

The safe answer was yes. She'd never gone to bed with a man on the first date. And this couldn't even qualify as that. But going to bed alone—again—had no appeal when there was such a stunning, sweet man before her. "No. Do you?"

His smile lit up the room. "No, I most certainly do not."

She slipped her hands under his shirt and lifted it over his head. Her breath caught as she stared at his chiseled abs and the dark hair that ran from just below his belly button under his jeans. He was amazing!

"You are beautiful." The compliment slipped between them, and Tessa wanted to slap herself. That wasn't a compliment for a man—was it? *Hot* or *handsome*—those were the words she should have used.

Nerves fluttered across her belly, and a heat that had nothing to do with Gabe's fingers stroking her arms cascaded across her. Max would have hated being called beautiful.

Striking was another word she could have used. Of course, now that the wrong word had slipped out, she could think of so many right ones. How could she be so out of practice at this?

"I mean—"

Gabe captured her lips before she could offer any explanation. When he pulled back, he ran a finger along her cheek. The gentle gesture made her bones melt.

"You're beautiful, too. So lovely."

The whispered words ignited deep inside her. It had been ages since anyone had called her beautiful.

Gabe's lips trailed along her neck. "I think we're both a little nervous."

"It's been a while," Tessa conceded.

"Well." His hands were warm as they slipped under her blouse. "What if we just go with what feels good?" His hand ran along the base of her bra, and Tessa's breath caught. "Does that feel good?"

"Yes." The breathy word echoed in the room, and Tessa let the worries slip away again. "But it's not enough." She yanked her shirt off and stood looking at Gabe, drinking in his admiration.

"Gorgeous." The tips of his lips curled up before he dipped his head to the top of her breast. "You are perfect, Tessa."

Perfect. That adjective had never been ascribed to her—at least not outside the hospital. But it pierced her, and a small part of her heart clasped it. Even if no one else ever said it again, she could treasure this one moment.

Her breath quickened and knees weakened as he dropped more kisses along the edge of her bra. The sensations scored across her as his fingers trailed ever closer to her nipple, but never quite close enough. Reaching behind her, Tessa unhooked her bra, reveling in Gabe's sigh as he gently sucked each of her nipples. The backs of her knees hit the bed, and she grinned as Gabe carefully laid her back.

His heated breath sent shivers along her skin as he slowly kissed his way down her stomach. He paused just above her waist and looked up. Their eyes connected. She unbuttoned the top of her skirt while he stared at her.

Was it possible to have such an instant connection with someone? To crave his touch?

His lips trailed fire as they traveled along the insides of her thighs. Her panties dropped to the floor, and she gripped the sheets.

"Tessa?"

When he lifted his head, Tessa sat up and grabbed the waistband of his pants. "It doesn't seem fair that I've lost all my clothes, and you haven't." His jeans slid to the floor, and she let her hands linger on his tight backside. He really was gorgeous.

As her fingers slid to the waistband of his boxers, Gabe gripped her wrist. "I want you, Tessa. Badly." He kissed the interruption from her lips. "But I still have plans."

"Plans?" Her heart skipped as she held his gaze.

His thumb grazed her nipple, and she shuddered. "I want to see you melt with pleasure." His fingers slid up her thigh, almost to her center but not quite. The heat scorched her, but it still wasn't enough. He licked each nipple before moving his way down her body—again.

Tessa arched as he drew closer to where she wanted him—needed him. "Gabe," she panted as he finally slipped a finger deep inside as his tongue teased her.

Dear God!

She wanted…needed more. "Gabe, please."

"Plans," the whispered word held so much promise as Gabe increased the pressure—barely.

Tessa arched again as waves of sensation crested over her. She lost herself in the feelings, the thrills his hands and mouth created as Gabe drove her closer and closer to the edge. "Gabe!"

Gripping his shoulders, she pulled him toward

her and captured his mouth as she slipped his boxers down. Had she ever wanted someone so badly?

She rolled him to his back and reached into the side drawer. The condom box was stuffed in the back. She'd purchased them a few years ago and found them in the box she'd simply labeled "nightstand" after moving in. It felt like forever, but when she finally slid down Gabe, her body took over.

His hands clasped her waist as he drove his hips toward her. Then he slipped his finger between them. The pressure made Tessa gasp.

"Tessa."

Her name on his lips was thrilling. "Gabe, Gabe... Gabe." His hips raised again, and Tessa crested into oblivion.

Tessa's breathing was light as he held her. Gabe pressed a soft kiss to her shoulder, simply relishing the feel of her next to him. He couldn't explain the rush of the connection between them, and he wasn't sure he wanted to.

Particularly after midnight. If he thought too much, he might rush from her bed. *Or get too comfortable.*

He ran his hand down her side. Her skin was so soft. The urge to touch her, to hold her, was burying itself deeper within him. Perhaps he should kiss her good-night and slip out—but that held absolutely no appeal.

He'd tried dating a few times since Olive passed, but his ability to feel connected to another had felt broken. Because he'd been broken.

He'd accepted that belonging to another person had ended—before it had even started, at least for him. Tragedy ripped away part of your soul, but he still had so much to be happy for. He might not be complete anymore, but being Uncle Gabe, a skilled nurse, an excellent brother and a good son was enough.

It was.

But tonight, he'd wanted more. Craved more. With Tessa, he'd felt almost whole for the first time in forever.

For a few precious hours, laughter had come easy—and it had been real. Not the forced chuckles that he'd become so adept at. He hadn't had to remind himself to smile. He'd simply enjoyed each moment.

Because of the woman beside him.

What did that mean? Probably nothing.

Gabe's heart skipped in his chest. He should just enjoy this time by her side.

She let out a soft sigh, and his name followed. *His name...*

Gabe's heartbeat felt like it echoed in the dark room. His soul cried at the small connection.

How did something so insignificant touch such a deep part of him?

"Tessa." His lips trailed along her neck.

Tessa moaned as his hand skimmed along her hip. She rolled over, and her dark gaze met his. Her eyes were hazy in the dim room, but the desire building there made him smile. *She* made him smile. *Tessa.*

"I didn't mean to wake you." The words were soft—and mostly true. He hadn't meant his touches to awaken her. But he wasn't sorry as her lips met his.

"I'm not sure I believe you." Tessa's long fingers stroked his chest, diving deeper with each exploration, "Did you want something?"

The question felt more profound than it should have, and Gabe's tongue was unable to form any reply. When her lips moved down his body, he let the question drift away in the fog of exultation.

Gabe's arm was heavy as Tessa slipped from the covers. His breath hitched, and all the flutters and questions she should have contemplated last night rushed toward her. The connection they'd had was electric, but she didn't know him. Not really.

They'd never even addressed the questions that one usually answered on a first date. *What do you do for a living? Hobbies? Future plans?*

No, they'd flirted over the weather. *The weather!* How had such a superficial conversation led to explosions in her bed?

Whatever had pulled at them, she needed a few moments of distance. Even though her body wanted her to wake the gorgeous, kind Adonis with kisses. And more.

So much more!

Pulling on a pair of shorts and a tank top, she headed for the kitchen. She needed coffee and a bit of space. What did one do the next morning? She'd never had a one-night stand.

But what if she didn't want this to be a one-night stand?

That thought sent thrills and panic racing through her. She and Gabe had an easy connection and chemistry that ignited desires deep within her. But that didn't necessarily mean anything.

She rubbed her arms, hating the uncertainty warring within her. Emotions were dangerous, and getting hurt seemed to be the natural order of the world. At least for the women in her family.

She stopped at the base of the steps and listened for any sign that the striking man was awake. The memory of his fingers running down her skin sent longing and heat rushing through her. But instead of returning to him, Tessa started for the kitchen.

Love was a chemical reaction. A dopamine high that vanished with time. She hated that thought, but her father had abandoned her mother when the family life he had claimed to need no longer excited him. And the high had evaporated years before Max had demanded a divorce.

Even with the pain it had witnessed, her heart still cried out for more. Maybe the organ was just a glutton for punishment as it whispered for her to consider that Gabe might be different?

Her phone buzzed, and Tessa frowned. She wasn't on call this weekend.

Dr. Lin told me he's retiring on our shift last night. His last day is in three months. His senior attending position should open in a few weeks. You're a shoo-in!

The text from Debra, the head nurse, made her smile. Tessa hopped from foot to foot. She wanted to burst with the news!

Now Tessa's heart was racing for another reason.

What would Gabe think?

She felt her lips tip down again. That errant thought was unacceptable. She'd known Gabe for six months when they were teens and now for one lovely night as adults. But she was not searching for the approval of any man regarding her career. *Not again.*

Tessa read the text again. *Senior attending...* Her skin bubbled with excitement. She wanted the promotion. It was the perfect chance to prove to herself that compromising her promotion in order to try to save her marriage hadn't dealt her career any setbacks.

She was the best choice, but that didn't always matter. She'd served as Dr. Lin's replacement when he'd had to have rotator cuff surgery last year, but she was younger than at least two other colleagues she knew would be interested.

And a woman.

Her gender shouldn't matter—but it did. She'd been asked questions throughout her career that her male colleagues had never faced. Particularly when it came to her plans to start a family.

People assumed her male colleagues had spouses, or ex-spouses, to look after their children. That they wouldn't need family leave. That they could operate at their best, even if they went home to a half a dozen children every night.

That wasn't an assumption that was granted to a woman of childbearing age. *No.* They had to prove that having a family wouldn't make them *less* of a physician.

For years, she'd said that she had no plans to start a family right away. There wouldn't be a need for maternity leave just yet. But she hated the answer. Hated being asked it. Hated answering it. Hated the emptiness that it always highlighted in her home.

She loved children. Tessa had never considered another specialty. Her mother had left med school after discovering she was pregnant with Tessa. Her dream had been permanently diverted, but she'd fostered Tessa's fascination with the human body and the healing arts.

Even as a teen, Tessa had known pediatrics was her calling. Taking care of children—big and little—made her happy. But it wasn't the same as coming home to a few of her own.

Rubbing her arms, Tessa tried to push away the pinch of unhappiness that always floated around her whenever she thought about how she had two extra rooms in this town house, and neither was a nursery or a playroom.

She'd always dreamed of having children. Of being the mom that hers hadn't gotten the chance to be. And she was sure she could be both an excellent mother *and* a wonderful doctor.

At least the question of a family was one she could answer easily now. With her divorce behind her, she wouldn't be having children anytime soon.

Maybe at all.

Pain sank into the room, and Tessa had to

force her lungs to expand. Biting her lip, Tessa closed her eyes and tried to focus on what she had. And how fulfilling those things were.

Her job. The prospect of a promotion. Her condo. Rediscovering herself after the divorce. She had more than many people. *Focus on the blessings you have.* Wallowing because everything she wanted hadn't come to fruition wouldn't make a family magically appear on her doorstep.

Her eyes wandered to the doorway. Last night's memory would always bring a smile to her lips. *Gabe.*

Tessa could fall for him, and that was terrifying. It would be nice to let the connection that had been so easy last night bloom. Get lost in his good heart and stunning dimples.

But there was always a cost to caring for someone. Her mother had paid the ultimate price for lost love. And if Tessa hadn't been so willing to make Max content, she would already be a senior attending.

No, Tessa wasn't prepared to pay for love and affection—not again. No matter how much a piece of her lonely heart cried out for it.

Dr. Killon is already talking about taking on extra shifts!

Debra's new text sent Tessa's eyes to the calendar. It was common for doctors to pad their résumés with extra shifts when coveted positions were opening. Luckily her calendar was completely clear. There was no one and nothing to stop her from working as much overtime as she could.

She looked at the empty last two weeks of the month and sighed. She should be excited that she didn't have to move anything around. That she could focus on this dream…but those blank dates highlighted a loneliness that cut deeper than she'd expected.

She lifted the page to look at the next month and stared at the block of leave she'd blotted out. She'd never worked on her birthday. Not out of any desire to celebrate the occasion; she hadn't celebrated the date since she was thirteen.

Tessa never did anything other than visit her mother's grave—which bore the date of Tessa's thirteenth birthday, too. But if the competition for the promotion was coming up, her mother would understand if Tessa broke that personal rule this year. After all, her mother hadn't gotten to chase her dreams—but Tessa could.

For both of them.

I can't wait to call you Boss!

That text forced away the pain.

Gripping the phone to her chest, Tessa spun around. She could do this. She could!

"Such a bright smile in the morning." Gabe grinned before his arms wrapped around her belly. Then he dropped a kiss to her cheek.

Maybe she didn't have to have an empty social life?

"A job that I have wanted for forever is finally coming open. My colleague was letting me know." Tessa brushed her lips against his.

"A job opportunity has you dancing around the kitchen this morning?" Gabe's voice dipped. His hands loosened on her hips.

Tessa tried to ignore the pinch of anxiety that pulsed in her back. *It's early and he hasn't had coffee. That wasn't a frown.*

These were the excuses she had lived with for so long with her ex. And she was not going to pepper them in this morning.

"Yes." Tessa nodded. "It's the thing I want most." That wasn't exactly true, but her connection with Gabe was too fresh to mention that she also wanted a family. A few kids to call her Mom. A happy home. Those desires were buried deeper—and harder to achieve than a promotion.

"A job," Gabe repeated before he shook his head.

This time he definitely frowned.

"Last night was fun." Tessa hated the words as they tripped from her lips. Fun didn't describe last night—or at least not completely. Amazing, rejuvenating, exciting…the start of something.

Except something had shifted in the morning light. Did he regret their night together? Or had the fact that she was excited about a promotion changed everything?

Gabe's phone buzzed, and he smiled as he read the message. "My sisters are not so patiently wondering where I am. We usually meet up for breakfast on Saturday." He pushed his hand through his hair.

Tessa gulped down the desire to ask if she could come. She would not tie her friends to a man again—even if Gabe remembered his offer to let his sisters adopt her last night. "It was good to see you again." Those words felt wrong, but she didn't know the protocol for this.

She grabbed the notepad sitting on her counter and quickly jotted her number down. Gabe looked at the note and smiled before pulling the pad from her fingers.

His touch still sent fire licking up her arms, but she had a terrible feeling that he wouldn't call.

And that would be fine.

Her heart sighed as he passed the notepad

back, his number scrawled across it. Then he pocketed her number. *Maybe he'll call after all.*

"I should probably get going." Gabe pursed his lips, looked at his phone, then back at her.

For a moment, she thought he might ask her to go. Instead, he dropped a light kiss to her cheek. After a night of passion, it crushed her.

But she was not going to let it show.

"It was good to see you, Gabe. Really." Tessa wrapped her arms around herself, the crumpled note with his number wrapped in her fist.

"It was good to see you too, Tessa." Gabe dropped another chaste kiss on her cheek, then he walked out.

CHAPTER THREE

PAPERWORK WAS NEVER-ENDING in the medical world. Tessa checked off another box on her tablet, trying to keep her mind from wandering to Gabe Davis. She'd alternately promised herself that she'd call him or throw his number away for the last two days. Not that throwing his number in the trash would offer her any relief.

She knew that number by heart now.

But every time her fingers hovered over the call button, the flicker of emotion he'd shown as she talked about the promotion stilled her fingers.

She'd seen a similar look before. Max had worn it for years. Before he'd given up the pretense that he didn't hate her success.

Gabe's face floated through her memory again, and Tessa wished, for the hundredth time, that that morning had gone differently. That he'd invited her to breakfast or asked when he could see her again instead of just exchanging numbers. That she hadn't witnessed the spark of uncertainty. That somehow their one night could transition to a fairy-tale story they'd tell their grandkids—minus a few details.

But life wasn't a fairy-tale. How often did she need to remind her heart of that?

Tessa's mother had married her father after a whirlwind romance. Less than four weeks after meeting her father, her mother had found out she was pregnant with Tessa. Her dreams of med school and becoming a surgeon had evaporated. But Tessa's father had immediately proposed and sworn he wanted to be a husband and father. That they could make it work.

He'd taken a promotion and moved their growing family from Houston to Dallas. Her mother's dreams had shifted from being a top physician to being the best wife and mother she could be. But it hadn't been easy. Tessa could still recall her practicing stitches on oranges—just for fun.

But they'd made do, and Tessa had never doubted that her mother loved her more than anything. Then her father had packed his bags to start a new business—one that he didn't want his wife or child to help him with. Last she'd heard, he was running a successful restaurant in upstate New York—with his fourth or fifth wife.

Her mother had believed in love. Even after setting aside her dream career to raise Tessa, and after her husband's abandonment. Even after taking on two jobs to make ends meet after her father's child support payments routinely failed to materialize. After watching her world implode, Tessa could still remember her mother saying that love was the most important thing. That it would all work out.

Except it hadn't.

Tessa had tried to take her mother's optimism into her own marriage, hopeful that she could have a love that lasted forever. But she hadn't gotten it, either.

Gabe wasn't Max or her father. At least, she was pretty sure he wasn't. But that dash of uncertainty she'd seen in his eyes had kept her from calling.

And he hadn't called, either. That stung.

"Dr. Garcia, have you met our newest pediatric nurse?" Debra, the head nurse on the unit, always walked the recent hires around, introducing them to their new colleagues. Most of the time, it didn't happen on their first day, and they already knew at least a few of their colleagues. But it was a Dallas Children's Hospital rite of passage. You weren't a full member of the staff until Debra had shown you off.

Tessa turned to smile at the new arrival, excited to focus on something besides paperwork or Gabe Davis. Her lips went numb. Gabe was standing next to Debra. She saw a glimmer of hesitation pass through his honey eyes before he offered a brilliant smile.

Had he missed her as much as she'd missed him? Why hadn't he called?

Neither of those were appropriate questions for the hospital.

"This is Dr. Tessa Garcia." Debra smiled at Gabe before turning her attention back to Tessa. "Nurse Gabe Davis."

"We met at a bar." The words blurted from her mouth. If there was a more embarrassing way for this reunion to go, she didn't want to find it.

Debra looked at her, and she saw the questions flickering in the woman's gaze. Tessa considered Debra a friend. She'd listened to her complaints when Max packed his bags and had declared him unworthy and suggested drinking away his memory. Tessa had thanked her, even enjoying the few jokes Debra had made. But lately, she'd been a little too interested in Tessa's lack of a dating life.

"What I mean—" Her cheeks were hot as she tried to find the right words, any words to follow her first statement as Debra cocked her eyebrow.

"We worked at a movie theater together in high school." Gabe turned the bright lights of his smile on Debra.

Tessa saw the happily married grandmother swoon.

"We ran into each other a few nights ago, and Tessa tried to convince me that the Dallas heat is preferable to the snowy locale I just came from."

"Snow!" Debra shook her head, horror drenching her features. "Not for me."

Tessa placed a hand against her cheek, grateful that it wasn't stinging with heat as she replayed where her last conversation about snow had led. Gabe's gaze met hers, and the draw she'd felt a few nights ago pulled at her. *He's here.*

"It's good to see you again, Tessa. I mean, Dr. Garcia. Always knew you were destined for great things!" His smile was deep as he nodded toward her.

His voice struck her, and Tessa barely kept from leaning toward him, her body aching with the memory of his touch. Her lips were desperate for one more kiss, even as her brain tried to remind her that he hadn't called.

"She *is* destined for great things!" Debra's voice echoed as she turned to lead Gabe away. "She's going to run this place someday—just wait and see." Debra looked over her shoulder and winked at Tessa.

Her stomach skittered and her body lit up as she let her gaze linger on him for a moment. How was she supposed to work with him?

By being a professional! Her brain screamed the command, but her heart wasn't sure. She'd certainly inherited her mother's romantic nature; unfortunately it hadn't earned either of them a happily-ever-after.

"I need help! Please!" The scream echoed from the room where a teenager was waiting on stitches following a skateboarding accident.

Gabe raced toward the room as the mother stepped out, carrying her younger daughter, his heavy footsteps pounding against the floor as he reached the mother.

"Please!" Her wail echoed down the halls.

Tessa saw several nurses motion for the other patients to stay in their areas—not an easy ask in a children's emergency room where little ones were already anxious and curious.

"Give her to me, please." Gabe's voice was firm as he reached for the young girl. His jaw tightened as he took the child. "Empty room?"

"Seven," a nurse from behind Tessa yelled.

Closing the distance between them, Gabe and Tessa quickly walked toward the empty room while another nurse tried to calm the mother enough to get details. "What do you think? I saw your face shift."

"Her breath is sweet. If she's in diabetic ketoacidosis, then we need—" Gabe dropped the statement as he laid the child in the bed. "Your orders, Doctor?"

Leaning over the small girl, Tessa could smell the sweetness of her breath, too. "Get me an IV line ready." She turned to the drawer and grabbed the blood-sugar-testing kit that was kept in each room. "Her blood glucose level is five-eight-six."

Any glucose level over four hundred was dangerous. But once you got over five hundred, you were dealing with a medical emergency. If they didn't get her sugar levels down, she could go into kidney failure or a diabetic coma.

Gabe nodded and immediately started working to secure a line in the girl's arm. A bag of fluids was hung on the hook. She looked so young and tiny in the bed as Tessa and Gabe worked to stabilize her.

"Her heart rate is steady." Tessa turned as Wendy, another nurse, walked in. "We need two units of insulin, and put another two on standby."

Wendy nodded and raced off.

The heart-rate monitor beeped, and Gabe looked over Tessa's shoulder. She knew he was making sure he knew exactly where the crash cart was. But they were not going to need that today. *Not today.*

A small sob echoed by the door, and Tessa turned. The girl's mom was standing just inside the threshold. "Do you have a history of diabetes in your family?" Her voice was steady but firm. People reacted to stress differently, but right now, they needed as many answers as possible.

The mother's eyes widened, and she shook her head. "No. No." She stifled another sob and squared her shoulders. Tessa had seen many parents do the same. Once the initial shock passed, they often fortified themselves to do whatever necessary for their children...and fell apart in the cafeteria when they were on a "coffee break" a few hours later.

"Okay," Tessa responded. Type one diabetes usually ran in families, but it could happen without any known genetic connection, too. "Has she been thirsty lately? Or complaining of headaches?"

Wendy stepped into the room and passed Gabe the insulin injections, then quietly took her place on the other side of the child's bed. A nurse's uncanny ability to enter the room silently or with as much ruckus as necessary depending on the situation never ceased to amaze Tessa.

"Rebecca is always thirsty. But the heat—" The woman's lip trembled. "I just thought—"

"This isn't your fault." Gabe's voice was firm as he triple-checked the line and readied the insulin injection that Tessa had ordered.

"Nurse Davis is right," Tessa agreed. "When you are fortunate not to have a history of diabetes in your family, often you learn by having your child fall unconscious. Luckily, your son was here already."

The woman wrapped her arms around herself as she stepped closer to the bed where her daughter was resting. "Will she be okay?"

"We've given her rapid-acting insulin. It will take around thirty minutes to take effect, but it should stabilize her. Then we'll monitor her blood sugar and use regular insulin to keep her stable." Tessa nodded toward Wendy. "Nurse Hill will stay and monitor her insulin every fifteen minutes for me. We have extra shots ready if necessary."

Tessa waited until Rebecca's mother looked at her. "Once her insulin comes back up, she will regain consciousness and likely be scared."

Her mother swallowed and then looked toward the door. "My son—"

The poor woman had been through too much today. This was one area where Tessa could alleviate a few of her worries. "I'll make sure your son's stitches are done, and he's sent in here. Rebecca will need to spend at least tonight with us, and we'll arrange for you to start counseling with the diabetic specialist tomorrow, too."

"Thank you." The woman wiped a tear away and slipped her hand into her daughter's.

Once they were in the hall, Tessa turned to Gabe. "Nice work. You saved us valuable time."

Gabe's gaze fell on the door to Rebecca's room, and a small shudder rippled across his shoulders. Tessa ached to rub the worry lines from his forehead.

She needed to get control of herself. They were at work; she should not be concerned with the tension radiating from him. But something about Gabe called to her.

"My sister Isla is diabetic. A few weeks after my mom left, Isla started complaining of head-aches. Dad was busy and…" His gaze flitted to the door as his voice died away.

"Anyway, we found out the same way they did—though we had to follow an ambulance and it took over an hour to figure out. She suffered permanent kidney damage. I will never forget the smell of ketoacidosis." He rocked back on his heels. "At least it saved us time today."

Tessa nodded, unsure what to say. The frown lines on his cheeks made her ache. As an only child, she couldn't really understand the close-ness Gabe had with his siblings, but she knew what it was like to be scared for someone you loved and unable to change anything. At least individuals with well-managed diabetes could live close to a normal life, though Rebecca would always need to make sure she was monitoring her body.

"Want to help me stitch up a skateboarder?" Tessa tapped her shoulder against his. It was a small connection, but her body vibrated as she pulled away. Apparently, even that friendly gesture was too much. *And not nearly enough!*

"Of course." Gabe's dimples hit her again.

Tessa felt a warmth slip through her. Any of the nurses could help with stitches. But Tessa wasn't ready to give up the time with Gabe. That was dangerous, but she didn't care. She was glad he was here. She'd wrangle her heart later.

Gabe's skin was on fire, and his mind was racing. Tessa was here. Here! If he focused, he could still feel the ghost of her touch on his shoulder.

His brain tried to keep his sprinting heart in check. He'd spent the last two days hoping she'd call, but nervous about pressing Send himself. When he'd come downstairs, he'd seen her do a little dance in the kitchen.

After their night together, Gabe's soul had soared that she might have enjoyed his presence as much as he'd enjoyed hers. That she might want to see what happened next.

And maybe she did!

But the excitement had been over a job—probably the senior attending position here. He'd worked two shifts and already heard multiple doctors and nurses discussing the potential opening.

His mother had danced in the kitchen like that once, too. He'd come down the morning before she packed her bags to see her swaying on the linoleum. She'd hugged him and told him that great things were coming. Except those things hadn't included her family.

She'd given him a list of things that needed done. And Gabe had done them. Hoping that he could earn a place in her new life.

Gabe was the only one who answered his mother's infrequent calls. She only ever called if she needed something, but Gabe hadn't given up hoping that she might want more of a relationship with him.

Tessa wasn't his mom—except she'd said this position was the thing she wanted most.

If Gabe was ranking his life goals, career progression would be on the list. Most people wanted to be successful. But it wouldn't be at the very top. Nothing would ever unseat his family.

But Gabe hadn't been able to drive away the longing to reach out to Tessa. He'd wanted to see if she might like to grab dinner, go hiking. He'd even wondered about the job she wanted. It had made her smile, a huge, warm smile, and he'd ached to know more.

He just longed to know Tessa. Gabe wasn't sure what to do with those feelings. But now wasn't the time to work through them.

"Ready?" Tessa's voice jolted him from his thoughts as she stopped in front of the door where he'd grabbed Rebecca.

"Is my sister going to be okay?" The boy's voice wavered, but he didn't break eye contact with Tessa as they stepped through the door. The teen's face had multiple abrasions, and his left arm was in a splint. He had to be in pain, but Gabe could see the worry coating him, too.

He'd worn that look often after his mom left. He'd worried over his father's exhausted features, over his siblings, over all the changes. It had taken him years to conquer the anxiety it created.

Then Olive had started complaining of headaches. She'd been so strong and independent. She'd blown it off as wedding and work stress, and he'd pushed away the worry that something was wrong, too.

Logically, Gabe knew that even if they'd discovered the aneurysm before it burst, there was little chance she'd have survived, given its location. But worry and guilt weren't things that you could easily wash away with logic.

And Gabe hated seeing it mirrored back to him with the young boy before him. There was nothing he could do for Olive now. But he could help the young man sitting on the exam table—after they addressed his visible wounds.

"Rebecca is going to be okay. But she's spending the night with the wonderful doctors and nurses upstairs."

Tessa's response released a bit of tension from the child's shoulders.

"Right now, though, Nurse Davis and I need to take care of you. Can you tell me your name?"

"Sam." The boy's lip trembled, but he stuck his chin out. "I want to see my sister."

"Not until we have you sewn up." Tessa smiled, but her voice was firm.

Even though the kid was still just a kid, he was at least three inches taller than Tessa and probably weighed at least fifty pounds more, too. But he looked so young as he glanced from Tessa to the door.

She examined his un-splinted arm before meeting the child's eyes. "I know you want to help your sister and your mom."

Tears welled in the boy's eyes, but he didn't drop his chin. "They need me. Dad's gone—" The statement was low and cut off by a sob he caught before it fully erupted.

"You can't help if you're not okay, Sam. Can't pour anything out of an empty cup." Tessa sat on the edge of the bed as she held up a light to examine the cut on his cheek. "I think we can just get by with a butterfly bandage on this one."

Gabe swallowed as she patted the boy's leg. The hospital was busy, but this was a child trying to be more than he was. Gabe understood that drive—and knew how tired Sam was. How tired he was going to continue to be. Tessa was taking extra time; making sure he knew that he mattered, too, was a balm that would soothe the boy for weeks, maybe even years to come.

Pediatric emergency room doctors were often judged on how quickly they fixed and released patients. And the metric was not weighted to give slow docs the advantage. At his last hospital a physician had been promoted because he was so efficient that his average time with a patient was less than twelve minutes.

It was not something Gabe thought should be rewarded. Stitches shouldn't take more than a few minutes. But Tessa was not rushing this simple interaction.

A lump formed in the back of his throat as Gabe pulled out the material for Tessa to stitch up the cuts on Sam's arm. That empty cup analogy was a line his sisters had repeated to him after Olive passed—when Gabe had tried to keep everything together while he was falling apart.

He'd been so used to helping others, to being needed, that he hadn't known how to ask for help—hadn't wanted it. Hadn't wanted to admit how lost he was.

That you can't keep trying to pour out of an empty cup was true. But following through with the sentiment was a lot harder for some people. And Gabe guessed Sam was like him. He would put everyone before himself and avoid his own wants—and needs—to make sure his mom and sister had as much as possible.

When Tessa stood to wash her hands, Gabe squatted, so he was looking Sam in the eye. "I know it feels selfish to put yourself first."

Gabe saw Tessa's head turn toward him out of the corner of his eye, but he kept his focus on Sam. "Anything you do for yourself, that makes you happy, takes time away from helping your mom and Rebecca, right?"

Sam sniffled and held up his splinted arm. "And it costs Mom money." He scowled at the appendage, and Gabe's heart broke. He'd crashed his skateboard. It was an accident, not a massive crime. But Gabe could see the loathing in the young man's eyes. That kind of thinking could worm its way deep inside and destroy so much.

"I've been there. I crashed my bike when I was seventeen. Ended up with a head injury, and it cost my dad almost a thousand dollars to make sure I hadn't cracked my skull." Gabe waited until Sam met his gaze before continuing, "But you're still a kid. A very helpful kid, I bet. But a kid. You aren't responsible for carrying everything. Dr. Garcia is right—you can't help if your well is completely drained. Trust me on that."

Pulling back, he watched Tessa stitch up Sam's arms. She talked in low tones about superhero movies and skateboards—two topics Gabe was stunned to realize she had so much knowledge of and was willing to spend time on. If metrics were being monitored for the senior attending position, too many extended interactions like this one could cost her. But she never cut off a question or rushed the stitches. They were going to heal with minimal scaring.

When the stitches were complete and she'd secured the bandage to his cheek, Tessa asked another nurse to walk Sam to his sister and mother.

"Gabe?"

He turned. Her dark eyes held such compassion *and* the emotions he'd seen the other night. Now was not the time to discuss what had happened between them, though. If Tessa wanted to talk, she had his number.

And he had hers.

"Do you think counseling would help Sam?"

Would it have helped you? That was the second question he saw dancing in her eyes. She might not realize the depth of his connection with the boy's circumstances—though maybe she did—but she'd seen it. The recognition of a soul trapped in the same cycle that caught many people in its lonely trap.

"I think so. But if money is tight—" Gabe shrugged. His father would have loved to have placed all his kids in counseling to deal with their mother's abandonment. Would have given them everything if he could have afforded it. "It will be the first thing to go if bills come due."

Tessa nodded and bit her lip. "I'll pull a favor from Dr. Gendler. With Dr. Lin retiring, everyone is looking for a leg up. He'll probably want—" Her words drifted away. "It's important that Sam get help."

So there would be a high price for the favor. "But you want the job, too." Gabe's voice was low as he stared at the woman across from him.

"Not at the cost of my patients." Tessa's eyebrows rose as she clicked through the tablet, closing out the notes on Sam's case. "No job is worth that."

His heart sang at that simple phrase, and he wanted to pummel himself. He should have called. Should have invited her to breakfast. Should have taken a risk.

But maybe it wasn't too late.

"This is quite the change of venue from the Tinseltown theater, huh? But it's nice to be working with you again, Gabe."

"You too, Dr. Garcia." Gabe beamed. "Dr. Garcia. That has a very nice ring to it, you know. It suits you."

The look she gave him lit up the hallway. "Thank you." Tessa let out a soft laugh. "That means a lot." She started toward the nurses' station before turning. "It really is good to see you here, Gabe."

There was a touch of something in the way she'd said his name, a softness that warmed his heart. For an organ that had been silent for so long, he wasn't certain exactly how to proceed now. His gaze locked on her as she walked away. Dr. Tessa Garcia. He smiled. Gabe was excited to be working with her again, too.

CHAPTER FOUR

TESSA JIGGLED HER tray and looked over the heads of individuals in the cafeteria. Dallas Children's pancakes were fan favorites, always drawing a larger number of staff and patients. But there was only one person she was looking for this morning.

Gabe...

Her body still lit with excitement and more than a touch of need whenever she was with him. They'd settled into a pattern of friendly chats when their shifts were slow. But it didn't sate Tessa's need to be near him.

The night of passion they'd spent together seemed to have been a fleeting moment. They never discussed it, though its presence seemed to hover in the rare uncomfortable silences that dogged their talks. And as each day ended, it seemed harder and harder to bring up.

But avoiding Gabe wasn't an option, either— at least not one that Tessa planned to exercise.

He'd burrowed deep inside her, and her heart refused to relinquish its quiet what-if questions. Though she tried to remind herself that she was done listening to that voice.

"You look deep in thought."

Gabe's warm tone ripped across her and she smiled.

God, she had it bad.

"What are you so focused on this morning?"

You. Tessa set her tray across from him and slid into her seat, determined not to mention that truth.

"Just thinking about how Dr. Lin hasn't even officially put in for retirement, and Dr. Killon is already lobbying for the job. He certainly has a high opinion of himself." Tessa carefully monitored Gabe's features, but he just plopped another bite of pancake in his mouth.

Gabe seemed to be the only employee uninterested in discussing which physician was the most likely replacement for Dr. Lin. Despite attempting to keep away from most of the talks, Tessa had been locked into more than a few gossip sessions regarding the future competition. Gabe's refusal to engage in the discussion was usually refreshing, but sometimes she really wanted to know his thoughts. *And whether he thought she'd be a good choice after working with her for a few weeks.*

This was an easy topic, though. Dr. Killon was inexperienced and showed little care for his patients. Gabe was still in his first month of employment, but he'd worked several shifts with the man. He was the last person anyone should want to replace Dr. Lin.

"Really, Gabe? No thoughts?" Tessa raised an eyebrow, hoping to draw some commentary from him on the job opening, wishing there were a simple way to know if her reaction to it was why he hadn't called.

His honey eyes held her gaze, and Tessa had to remind herself to breathe.

"Tessa—"

Before he could finish that statement, something hot and sticky slid down Tessa's back. The heated syrup burned a line down her spine.

Then hands pushed into her, and a tray clacked to the floor. The owner of the liquid fell to the ground.

A cry of alarm echoed in the crowded cafeteria as Tessa turned to find a teen seizing.

She moved quickly. Pushing back at the curious onlookers who were gathering, Tessa slipped next to the young man's side. She heard creaking and looked up to see Gabe climbing over the table to reach her and the patient. That was an effective way to get through a gathering crowd.

"Help me turn him on his side." Tessa nodded to Gabe as he helped shift the boy. Then her eyes went to her wrist. They needed as accurate a time count as possible.

"Make way!" a voice called.

Debra and Jackson stood by with the portable crash cart. Tessa turned so she could keep a better focus on her patient and her watch. The longer the seizure went on, the more likely the teen was to suffer long-term consequences.

Or need the crash cart.

The minute hand moved on her watch, and Tessa heard Gabe let out a soft sigh. She briefly looked to him. A bead of sweat coated his upper lip, and his shoulders were rocking. But he did not let his gaze leave their patient.

Blessedly, the boy started to release. *Thank goodness.*

"One minute, twenty-eight seconds." Gabe's voice was ragged as he sat back on his heels to let the gurney through.

"I got the same," Tessa stated. Gabe's hands were shaking. *What was going on?*

Something about this patient had impacted Gabe. There was too much for her to focus on. But as soon as she knew their patient was going to be all right, Tessa was going to find Gabe. Whatever memory this had dredged up, he needed someone. And that was something she could offer him.

* * *

Gabe's body swung between hot and cold flashes as he leaned against the wall in the employee lounge. He'd helped patch up a little girl who'd fallen from her bike and needed stitches, and delivered discharge papers to another, but his mind kept wandering to the closed doors where Tessa and others were dealing with the seizure patient.

The teen had briefly met his gaze before he dropped hot syrup down Tessa's back. The world had stopped, and his breath had caught in his throat. He hadn't even been able to find the words to call out a warning. His lips had been frozen as the past raced through him.

The unfocused eyes. The drifting step. The crash. Olive had experienced each of those symptoms in quick succession the morning he'd lost her.

The aneurysm that had plucked her away had bulged, pressing on a nerve, resulting in a seizure. Then it had ruptured.

Gabe knew the odds that a boy who couldn't be over seventeen was having a seizure because of an aneurysm were minuscule. Those types of clots almost always built up over a long lifetime. But Olive had been vibrant, independent and twenty-six when one had stolen her away. There were no guarantees in this world.

"Gabe."

Tessa's soft voice sent skitters across his raw nerves. The present overtook the past as he pushed away from the wall.

"He's all right." She didn't waste any words as she stepped toward him, her face open and concerned—for Gabe.

"Did he have an MRI?" Gabe's voice sounded off, and he crossed his arms. Olive had been fine for a precious hour after she'd seized. He'd sat next to her in the ER, trying to keep her spirits up as worries mounted. When she'd screamed from the pressure suddenly pressing through her skull, Gabe had known what it meant.

And been unable to do anything other than hold her hand as she slipped away.

Tessa's gaze flickered, and Gabe wondered if she could see the roller coaster rushing through him.

"No, I didn't order an MRI." She kept her voice calm as she carefully watched him. "You're so pale." She took a deep breath and placed a hand on his chest as she held his gaze. "Breathe with me." She inhaled, held it for a second, then waited for him to follow her.

Her soft scent chased through him as the present pushed the past's panic aside. His heart raced, but that was because of Tessa's light touch. When she stepped away, he hated the distance between them.

"He's an epileptic. The new medication his neurologist prescribed is not managing it as well as hoped. He was actually here under observation as they weaned him off it and restarted his old regimen. He got hungry and went for pancakes without asking.

"Teens, right?" She let out a soft laugh.

The sound sent a touch of longing through him. For the hundredth time, he wished he'd called her. That he hadn't let his fear still his fingers.

"I'm glad he's all right."

"Your girlfriend died of a seizure?" Tessa followed Gabe to the small window, her presence sending a wave of contentedness through him.

Gabe swallowed the twisting emotions as he stared out at the parking lot. He would always miss Olive. There was a hole in his heart that no one could fill. You learned to accept that a piece of you was gone, but grief transformed. It morphed. It became easier to hold others, to think about opening yourself up to another. At least that was what the books he'd been given following Olive's passing had said.

He hadn't felt that…until he met Tessa. Today the past had flitted into his future, and it hadn't been the debilitating pain of her loss that had driven his concern over the teenager. It was the aftermath that Gabe feared for another family.

As a pediatric nurse, he'd helped stabilize many seizure patients, but usually after the seizure started. Witnessing the start had thrown him because the teen had so perfectly mimicked her symptoms.

"Olive was my fiancée." Gabe let out a breath and squeezed Tessa's hand, grateful that she had seen how the episode had affected him. And sought him out.

"But I lost her to a brain aneurysm. She seized about two hours before. The symptoms were identical to the teen before…" He let the last words go unsaid. "I'm glad the patient is going to be all right."

"Winston. His name is Winston."

"Of course you know his name." Gabe forced himself to release the pocket of air he'd been holding.

A frown line creased Tessa's forehead. "Of course. I just left his room, Gabe."

"True." He offered a smile. "But not every doctor focuses so closely on their patient. I suspect if Dr. Killon had treated him, he wouldn't be able to tell me his name. He also wouldn't have noticed someone else's distress."

Gabe had heard all the rumors regarding Dr. Lin's position. The man hadn't even officially put in his retirement request, and people were acting as though his last day had already occurred. Gabe hadn't wanted to feed into that rumor mill but when Tessa had asked him about Dr. Killon this morning, he should have responded.

Should have joked that he didn't want to see the man running anything—anywhere. They were colleagues and friends now—a little workplace discussion about something Tessa cared about should have occurred.

The tips of her lips twisted up.

He enjoyed seeing her happy.

"That's true," she conceded, "but he would have correctly diagnosed his problems."

"Yes." Gabe took a deep breath and looked into the dark eyes that called to him. "But a senior attending should care about more than just the condition."

The look of joy that flitted across her face made Gabe wish he knew a way to bridge the gap that had opened since the night he'd spent at her place.

He wanted more than passing conversations in the hallway. More than the friendly waves and smiles. So what if she was interested in a promotion? That didn't mean that she'd choose it over everything else. She cared about her patients, and the staff.

His mother only cared about herself. She never

looked at others as anything other than pawns to help drive her own desires. He'd let his fear keep him from seeking something that made him happy.

"How's your back?" It wasn't the question Gabe wished to ask, but he'd find a better place than the hospital break room to ask her out. *And soon.*

"Sticky." Tessa laughed as she stepped to her locker. "Very sticky!"

Tessa stepped into the elevator and leaned against the wall. Her day hadn't been terrible, but she'd run from patient to patient with no downtime. Her toes ached in her shoes. She was looking forward to comfy socks and an easy evening.

"Hold the elevator!"

Tessa put her hand to the door, stopping the sensor. Fingers grazed hers before pulling back, but her body lit with recognition. *Gabe.*

"Thanks." He grinned as he stepped into the elevator with her.

He leaned on the other wall, several feet from her, but Tessa's body called out at the close confines, aching to bridge the distance. To see what he'd do if she invited him to dinner.

It would be nice to have someone over to dinner. To have a house with noise that didn't just come from the television. To spend time with people outside the hospital.

To spend time with Gabe.

Swallowing those desires, she shifted her messenger bag. "No problem. I know what it's like to want to get home. A little peace and quiet after the craziness here."

Gabe shrugged. "That might be nice, but I'm still couch surfing at my sister's place. Stacy's girls don't really do peace and quiet."

That would be nice to come home to, too. Sticky faces and loud noises. Belonging. *Family.* Tessa pushed that need away before she could mention that she'd love to come home to sticky faces and loud noises. No need to further embarrass herself.

"I'm constantly fending off her oldest's karate moves. She may be almost two feet shorter than me, but I am pretty sure Brett could pin me with ease!"

Tessa laughed as the elevator doors opened to the parking garage, wishing she could extend the interval with Gabe. He always found ways to make her smile. Real smiles, not the fake fixtures that had become her mask during the final years of her marriage.

"I'd love to watch you dodge her. I bet it's a

sight to see." Tessa caught the desire to ask if she could come over sometime—but barely.

Get it together!

Her body heated as Gabe's dark gaze held hers. He cleared his throat and stepped from the elevator.

Gabe turned. "What are your evening plans?"

Her stomach flipped as she shrugged. "Reading up on hydroponic gardening." *Nothing that can't be rescheduled.*

His dimples appeared as he stared at her. Hope fluttered in the dimly lit garage.

Gabe put his hands into the front pocket of his backpack and pulled out a set of keys. "How—" His faced shifted as he looked away. "That sounds interesting. I'd like to hear more about it sometime."

An awkward pause erupted between them. Time extended as she looked at his chiseled features.

Why didn't you call? The question reverberated around her brain as they stood together.

The elevator dinged behind her and the spell binding them broke.

"Have a good night, Tessa and Gabe," Debra shouted as she walked toward her car.

"You, too!" Gabe called as Tessa waved.

"Enjoy your book." Gabe tipped his head as he spun his keys around his fingers.

"Watch your back around your niece." Tessa pulled her keys from her bag, too.

His deep chuckle sent need cascading through her.

"Always." He winked and walked away.

She let out a breath, trying to calm her heart rate.

Want to get dinner? See a movie? Why were those phrases so hard to utter? If he said no, Tessa would at least know.

But no also meant he really wasn't interested—and she wasn't ready to lose the bright bit of hope her heart was clinging to.

"I'm headed to the coffee shop. Do you want me to grab you something?" Tessa offered as she stepped out of a patient's room.

"I'd kill for an iced caramel macchiato!" Gabe's step picked up as he moved beside her. He still hadn't figured out the perfect way to ask her out. It should be simple. *Want to grab dinner?* But he wanted it to be…*epic.*

To be something she wouldn't turn down.

Tessa grinned, but her eyes weren't as bright as they normally were when she met his gaze before she offered a pretend shudder. "I asked if you wanted coffee. Not a cup of sugar."

He loved sweet drinks, but it was the company Gabe craved, not caffeine. He leaned as close as he could in the hospital and whispered, "You might like it if you tried it."

The twitch in her lips lifted his spirits even further. He was happy when he was with her.

"I think I'll stick to my regular."

Gabe shuddered as she winked, the playful exchange putting an extra bounce in his step. How Tessa gulped down cup after cup of black coffee was beyond him. He might like and sometimes need the caffeine boost, but it could be done with a little chocolate or caramel drizzle!

"Any word on the job?" Gabe tried to keep the question light. He'd never understand the craze this position was causing among the doctors. But he was trying to be supportive. It mattered to Tessa.

And she'd be great at it. Gabe knew that, but he was still concerned that she was pushing herself to the edge. Over the last few weeks, she'd been at the hospital during each of his shifts. And on most of the days he wasn't here, too, according to the other nurses.

It was one thing to love your job, to want the best for your patients—Gabe understood that drive because it rumbled through him, too—but living at your job, focusing only on it, was a recipe for disaster. But he wasn't sure how to bring up the worry—or if it was even his place.

But surely a friend could point out that Dallas Children's Hospital was not a person. That it couldn't love its employees. When one moved on, another would be hired. Even Dr. Lin, who'd been a senior attending for almost a decade and a half, could be replaced easily enough. Shoot, people were talking about his replacement before he'd officially announced his last day.

"No word." Tessa frowned as they reached the coffee shop.

The line was longer today than usual but Gabe didn't mind. A few extra minutes with the woman beside him was a joy.

"I'm worried they might look to an outside hire." She pressed her fingers to her lips.

Gabe bumped his shoulder against hers, hating the dip of concern he saw floating in her features. Dr. Lin had only told a few people he was retiring; he hadn't made anything official. There was nothing the hospital could do yet.

"Not that Human Resources will ask me, but I think hiring one of our doctors would be best."

"You'd be a good resource for them." Tessa looked at her hands before meeting his gaze. Emotion floated there that made his knees weak.

Did she feel the electricity that connected them, too? Did she still lie awake at night thinking of their time together?

Tessa leaned a little closer, and her scent made

Gabe want something very different from caffeine.

"You notice things. You listen better than anyone I've ever met, and you genuinely care about the patients and staff. Actually, you probably care about everyone you meet."

"Life's too short not to make everyone feel special." Gabe grinned. A look passed over her face that he couldn't quite understand. Before he could ask, they'd reached the front of the line.

"Happy birthday, Dr. Garcia." A resident waved and raised his coffee toward them.

Birthday? Why hadn't she'd said something? The hollow in his belly expanded. He'd have gotten her a card.

Or used it as an excuse to plan a birthday dinner. It would have been the perfect opportunity to see if she wanted to test out the feelings that still seemed to crackle between them.

"Thanks." Tessa waved before staring at her shoes.

"Well, let me buy the coffee today. After all, I didn't realize we were celebrating." Gabe ached to throw an arm around her shoulder, but that was too much. *And yet not enough.*

"We aren't." Tessa's words were tight, and the flinch along her jaw nearly stilled his feet.

What had he said? Gabe hated the tension stringing through her. "Tessa?"

"Medium house blend, black." She held her badge up to the scanner and stepped aside to let him order his drink without looking at him.

"Large caramel macchiato with an extra shot of espresso." Gabe pressed his badge to the scanner, too, before moving to her side. Her lips were pursed, and her gaze was far away. What was he missing?

Birthdays should be a day of celebration.

His father had always made a big deal of birthdays. Even when money had been tight, a birthday cake decorated in the birthday boy's or girl's favorite color always materialized on the hand-me-down kitchen table. Balloons purchased from the Dollar Store were taped to the wall, and the entire family sang to—or rather belted at—the newly aged member of the group.

Even now, his siblings had a tradition of trying to be the first to call on someone's birthday. The silly tradition had gotten so out of hand that a few years ago, a truce had been declared that no one could start the call until at least five in the morning in whatever time zone the birthday person was in. Only Gabe and Isla still competed to be first, but that was because Matt and Stacy preferred to sleep until a reasonable hour now that they were settling down with kids.

"So, you don't like your birthday?" Gabe grabbed his large drink and took a deep sip.

"No." Tessa lifted the coffee to her lips, but it didn't mask the subtle shake in her hands.

Most of the medical professionals Gabe knew didn't mind adding years. Once you saw how fragile life really was, you celebrated the additional laugh lines and crow's-feet that far too many people never got to earn.

"You want to talk about it?" He knew the answer before the question left his lips, but he didn't regret asking it. Gabe wanted to know about Tessa, and he wanted her to know that he wanted to know her.

"No." The word was clipped, but he saw the twitch of her lips behind the cup. It wasn't much, but at least she knew he'd listen if she opened up about it.

She grimaced and ran a hand along her belly.

"Seriously, are you okay?" Gabe reached for her elbow as she shuddered. She had been working extra shifts; he knew how much exhaustion could bring emotions to the surface. What was going on?

"I think coffee in the afternoon just isn't sitting right with me." Her jaw clenched as she looked at the cup. "Maybe it's because I'm getting older." Tessa winked.

His chest seized as her dark eyes held his. This wasn't the place he'd planned or the perfect moment he wanted, but Gabe was done waiting. "How about we—"

"Code yellow! Code yellow!"

Tessa's eyes flew to the speaker on the wall before her feet took off.

Gabe dropped his full drink into the trash can beside the emergency room's side door. Adrenaline raced through him, but it didn't push away all the concern for the woman who hit the ER doors a second before he did.

"Seven-car pileup on I-635. At least four of the cars had families. We've got six patients incoming. More possible!" The call came up from the nurses' station, and Gabe saw the color drain from Tessa's face before she squared her shoulders.

They'd had a few bad days since he'd started working at Dallas Children's. It was always difficult when you had more than broken bones and stitches, but her panicked look as the nurse stated that the adults were heading to Presbyterian Hospital sent a chill down his spine. This was one of the worst ways to spend your birthday.

She hated this day! If there were happy memories tied to it, Tessa couldn't dredge them up.

"Where is my momma?"

The tiny voice belonged to Natalie Dreamer, the final patient on Tessa's long list of little ones who had been on Interstate 635. A church group had been carpooling to a campout. An elderly driver suffered a cardiac event and crossed three lanes of traffic. Seven of the fifteen cars in the caravan had been involved in the resulting pileup.

Bending to look at the dark-haired cutie, Tessa tried to keep her voice even. All she knew was that Natalie's father was on his way here, and her mother was at Presbyterian Hospital.

Please… Tessa sent the tiny plea into the universe, hoping that this might be the one time it listened to her entreaties. Tessa didn't want to add another tragedy to today's list of traumas. *Please…*

"Your dad will be here shortly, Natalie." Tessa smiled, hoping it seemed comforting. She'd been this child once, asked everyone where her mother was. All the smiles she'd been offered that day hadn't mattered as she'd sat in the waiting room with a tiny stuffed elephant that a nurse had procured from the gift shop. She'd clung to it, even though she'd sworn off stuffed animals as babyish in a fit of preteen drama the year she'd turned twelve.

It was the last birthday present she'd allowed herself to receive.

The door to the room opened and Gabe stepped in. His eyes were heavy with exhaustion, but he offered a bright smile to Natalie. Then he pulled a pink bunny from behind his back. Tessa couldn't quite control her recoil.

Gabe's gaze darted toward her before returning to Natalie. He was very perceptive, but Tessa hoped he'd just think she was tired. Which she was.

No matter how much sleep Tessa got lately, it was never enough. But that was a problem for another day, too. *Focus!*

"Bunny!" Natalie grabbed the stuffed animal, snuggling it close with the arm that wasn't in a sling.

"I thought it might help to have a snuggle partner while Dr. Garcia puts your arm in a cast." Gabe made sure he was at Natalie's level as he addressed the child. It was a small thing, but children often felt more comfortable when an adult was at their level. Even after treating their share of the fifteen patients who had arrived from the car accident, Gabe didn't rush through his patient interactions.

He'd make an excellent partner and father.

The loose thought stunned Tessa as she prepared the material for Natalie's fiberglass cast. Mentally shaking herself, Tessa tried to focus on the task in front of her. But if you worked in a children's hospital, you saw more broken bones than probably any other medical professional, so she could do this routine in her sleep.

She should be thrilled that Gabe was such an excellent pediatric nurse—that he fit so well at Dallas Children's. Little boys needed to see men in caring roles—needed to know they could become nurses, too. That it wasn't just a girl job.

But Tessa wanted more than coffee runs and break-room chats. There'd been a few times when she'd thought he was about to ask her out. Like that evening in the parking garage. But the topic always seemed to shift to something else.

Usually a question regarding Dr. Lin's position. Tessa felt her lips turn down and tried to wipe the emotion from her face. She'd been thrilled when Gabe had finally started talking with her about the job, but after previously ignoring the topic, he now broached it at least once every other shift.

Was that why he hadn't asked her out? Tessa didn't want to believe that. But she hadn't wanted to believe that her ex-husband was jealous of her, either.

She could ask him out. It was the twenty-first century. Women did that. But each time she'd considered it, her tongue had failed to deliver the words.

If he said no, she was afraid she'd lose what they had now. An easy work relationship wasn't all she wanted, but it was better than awkward silence. When he was around, Tessa didn't feel so unmoored in the world, a sensation she hadn't realized was so normal until Gabe's anchor had appeared.

Gabe's anchor? That was romantic fairy-tale stuff that rarely led to happily-ever-after. They'd had one perfect night, but that did not qualify as an anchor.

But as she looked over at him, Tessa's nerves and aching heart calmed slightly. Breathing through the pain of today was easier when he met her gaze.

"Will my cast be really pink?" Natalie's voice was soft, but it broke through Tessa's mental musings.

"Really, really pink—" Tessa grinned "—with sparkles." Having a broken bone wasn't a cause for celebration, but many kids got excited to have a fun color.

"Sparkles?" Gabe opened his mouth, pretending to be shocked by the revelation. Most of the girls who broke a limb asked for sparkle casts and many of the boys, too. Sparkles could make almost anything better. "Now I wish I had a sparkle cast."

"It hurts to get one." Natalie's eyes were damp with unshed tears as she looked toward Gabe. "I wish Momma was here."

A lump stuck in the back of Tessa's throat. Her gaze flitted to Gabe, willing him to understand that she couldn't answer. She must be more exhausted than she'd realized. Tears threatened to spill into her eyes, too, as she looked at the young girl. She bore so many similarities to Tessa. What if today she joined the terrible club that no child should have a membership to?

Gabe sat on the table with Natalie and tapped the top of her bunny's ears to get her attention. "I called the other hospital before I came in. I have an old friend who works there. Your mommy is going to have to stay with them for a few days, but she is okay." He raised his eyes to meet Tessa's and repeated, "She's okay."

Tessa wasn't sure what strings he'd pulled to get that information, but she was grateful as she watched Natalie exhale. He'd given her the best gift possible. And a pink bunny, too!

"So, let's get your pink sparkle cast ready. That way, when your dad gets here, he can take you to see your mom." Tessa made the statement, then caught her breath. Gabe hadn't said what condition Natalie's mom was in, but she couldn't pull the words back now.

"That cast is a genuine work of beauty." Gabe grinned as Natalie held it up for inspection.

"Yes, it is," a man who looked strikingly like the little girl stated as he stepped through the door.

"Daddy!" Natalie hopped off the bed. "Look

what Nurse Davis got for me!" She held the bunny next to her cast. "They're both pink."

"Imagine that." He bent and pulled his daughter close.

Tessa saw him tremble a little as he kissed the top of her head. The ache in her chest opened further as she watched Natalie's father hold her. Tessa's father had been gone for years when she'd lost her mother. She'd never gotten the hugs and comfort that Natalie's father could give her.

Tessa's grandmother had tried, but she'd been consumed with the grief of losing her only child and the added responsibilities of raising her granddaughter. She'd exited retired life, reentered the workforce and done her best for Tessa. But she hadn't been her mother.

The last person who'd held Tessa like that had been gone twenty-three years now. And this year, Tessa was officially older than her mother had ever gotten the chance to be.

"Her mom?"

Tessa felt the words leave her lips. There was no way to recapture them—but even if she could, she wanted to hear that the little girl's mom was all right. If it had been any other day, any other situation, she'd never have asked. But she wanted the confirmation that she'd never gotten as a child.

"Yes, where's Mommy?" Natalie bounced,

trying to break the tight hold her father had. She was too little to understand how much he must need to touch her. To convince himself that his little girl was indeed all right—mostly.

"Mommy has broken bones like you. In her left leg. She's going to have to stay in the hospital for a few days, and she'll be in a bigger cast than you." Natalie's dad brushed a piece of hair from her cheek.

"Is hers pink, too?"

Her dad chuckled as he shook his head. "I bet she wishes it was. But nope. Just a plain white cast."

Gabe made a motion to Tessa, and she nodded to him. They needed to give this little family a few minutes together. Just before she closed the door, Tessa turned and looked at the father and daughter. Their embrace sent chills through her. How much she yearned for just the comfort of a hug. The comfort of knowing there was someone who noticed that she wasn't okay. A little wish that was so far out of reach.

CHAPTER FIVE

GABE STOOD IN front of Tessa's town house holding a box of cupcakes, hoping she wouldn't care
that he'd just shown up. He'd tried to catch her
after their shifts ended, but she'd vanished the
second they could clock out. So he'd grabbed
the box of cupcakes from a bakery by his sister's house, raced to Stacy's, showered and then
come here.

He wasn't sure what was going on, but Gabe
needed to see that she was okay. Something
about the accident on the highway had touched
Tessa more deeply than a stack of badly injured
patients. That was not the memory that Gabe was
going to let linger on her birthday.

Besides, even if they hated the day, no one
should be alone on their birthday. Particularly
after a day like today.

Medical professionals faced more bad days
than most. It was a career field ripe with im-
pressive highs. They occasionally got to witness

miracles, but those highs came with devastating lows when the unthinkable occurred. Medical staffers were forced to develop coping mechanisms.

He always spent more time lifting weights when the weeks were going poorly. Not because lifting heavy things made him feel better, but because the pain in his aching muscles drowned out the other racing thoughts. And pushing his body made him feel a little more invincible in a world where invincibility was a true illusion.

He didn't know Tessa's self-care routine, but whatever it was, she shouldn't do it alone. *Not today.*

The tears in Tessa's eyes as she watched Natalie hug her dad had cut across Gabe's heart. Tessa was hurting—aching—and he longed to reach out to her. But there wasn't an easy option at the hospital.

She needed someone. And he was done waiting for the perfect time. He was here for her—in any way she wanted.

Gabe was lucky. He had his family to walk beside him when the world turned upside down. She'd told him on the first night he'd seen her that there was no one in her life to protect her. No one to shoulder the trauma that a day like today would bring. It had troubled him then.

But it pulled at him now. If she'd let him, maybe Gabe could be that person.

Nerves chased up his spine as he made his way to her door. He wanted to be the shoulder she cried on, the one she danced in the kitchen with, the one who made her laugh and smile.

But if Tessa didn't want the same, he'd find a way to settle for being her friend. Tessa belonged in his life. He was certain of that.

The chime echoed through the door, and Gabe straightened his shoulders as his stomach flopped with nervous and excited energy.

"Just a moment." Tessa's voice sounded strange on the other side of the door, or maybe it was just the door making it sound like it was breaking up. His heart burned as he waited for her to open the barrier between them.

"Gabe?" Tessa's voice shook, and her cheeks were tearstained when her gaze met his. "What are you—" Her gaze floated to the pink box in his hand. "Are those Maggie's cupcakes?"

"Yes." The tear streaks worried him. How long had she been crying? Maybe he shouldn't have taken the detour for pastries.

But her gaze brightened as she leaned toward the pink box. He flipped the lid open, and his soul eased as Tessa's body relaxed some.

He hadn't known which flavor was her favorite, so each of the cupcakes was different. They made a pretty display in the bubble gum–colored box. If the confectionery treats got him in the door to help her, he'd frequent Maggie's bakery more often. His nieces and nephews would love that!

"You didn't have to bring me cupcakes." Tessa offered a weak smile as she stepped back to let him in. "But I'm glad you're here."

"Today was rough." Gabe looked over his shoulder as he headed toward her kitchen. "You ran out before I could check on you. So…" He shrugged. "Figured a sweet treat might soothe away a few of the day's rough edges."

"So this isn't a birthday celebration?" Tessa cocked her head as she stared at him.

Raising his right hand, he grinned. "I promise these are only half birthday treats."

She let out a light chuckle as she grabbed the coffee cupcake and held it up. "Only half? So what's the other half?"

"You seemed upset earlier. So these are 'make sure Tessa is okay' treats." Gabe studied her as she sat across from him. Her eyes were red, and there were exhaustion pockets under them. She was tired and sad, and he was here to relieve as many burdens as she wanted to drop at his feet.

Tessa mattered to him. And he wanted her to know that. Needed her to know that.

"My mom died today." Tessa let out a soft

sob as she pulled the wrapper off her cupcake. Her fingers trembled, and she set the cupcake down on its paper wrapper. Like she was afraid the confectionery wonder might tip out of her shaky grip.

Gabe's tongue was momentarily frozen as he tried to process that statement. What had she been doing at the hospital today?

"What can I do?" Gabe reached for her hand. His heartbeat steadied as her long fingers wrapped around his. He hoped he had the same calming effect on her that she had on him.

"Oh." Tessa squeezed his palm, and she didn't let go. "I meant this is the anniversary of her death. It's been twenty-three years. But this—"

She blew out a breath and stared at her ceiling for a second, trying to compose herself, like there was any shame in mourning someone years after they'd departed. He still took the day off on the anniversary of Olive's passing.

"It's okay." His thumb rubbed along the delicate skin just below her wrist. He knew what small connections to others meant. How it grounded you when it felt like everything else in the world was unhinged.

She ran her free hand under her nose and shook her head. "I'm not usually such a watering pot. I swear. I guess…" She shrugged and looked out the window. "I'm older than her today.

Every birthday, starting with this one, marks a year she never saw. It feels weird. That probably sounds silly."

"No." Gabe let go of her hand and moved around the counter. He pulled her into his arms and just held her. She let out another sob, and then another as he tightened his grip. She laid her head against his shoulder, and he felt the tension melt from her shoulders. He'd hold her for as long as she needed.

After several minutes, she let out a deep breath and pulled back. "Thanks. I needed that hug. But this is probably not what you expected when you brought cupcakes over." She tried to smile as she headed back to her seat, but only the tips of her lips moved. She reached for her cupcake and took a big bite.

"These are so good." She let out a sigh, but no tears hovered in her eyes.

"Happy to help. I'm here for you." Gabe waited until she met his gaze. "Any time you need it. I am here, hugs and all."

"Thank you." Tessa lifted the cake to her lips. "To sugar and—" her cheeks darkening "—friends."

Gabe swallowed the knot in his throat as he grabbed the double chocolate cupcake. That wasn't the term he wanted to use. But he wasn't going to push, at least not tonight.

She took a big bite of the pastry. "I love Maggie's!" She quickly finished the treat and looked at the box. "It's my birthday, and I am having another."

She sighed before grabbing the lemon cupcake. "I usually take the day off at the hospital. But with Dr. Lin's job potentially opening, everything gets monitored, discussed…dissected. I didn't want to take any unnecessary leave."

Unnecessary leave?

Recharging yourself on a difficult anniversary was not something he'd describe as unnecessary. He knew Tessa was interested in the job, but she still had years left at the hospital. If she didn't get the position, others would open. Why the focus on this one?

"Today is always difficult. But the accident—" Tessa's words drifted away as she met his gaze.

"You lost her in a car accident?"

Tessa spun the lemon cupcake around. Her gaze focused on the edible pearl beads decorating the light yellow frosting. Her mind seemed a million miles away, but Gabe wasn't going to draw her back. She'd tell him in her own time—or she wouldn't. Either way, he was here for her.

"She had two jobs, and she'd worked sixteen hours a day for almost two weeks. After my father left us, the bills were piled high and—" Another tear spilled down her cheek as she raised her eyes to meet his.

"Mom fell asleep. For just a minute, but that was enough. We drifted across two lanes of traffic. I screamed. She woke, but it was too late to course-correct. Twenty-three years ago, I waited at Dallas Children's with a broken arm, clutching a stuffed elephant that a nurse procured for me. Except when my grandma came to get me, my mom was gone." She hiccuped as she shook her head.

"I should have told Mom it was all right that I didn't have a birthday cake or present. That we didn't need to go get anything. Not that it would have mattered." Tessa hugged herself and sighed. "She didn't want her daughter to miss out on the birthday fun. She was a very determined woman. And caring."

"Just like her daughter." He was glad she had such fond memories of her mother. That the traits she used could so easily describe Tessa, too. "I'm sure she would be proud of everything you've done."

She pulled at the collar of her deep blue T-shirt before dipping her finger in the frosting and lifting it to her lips. "I like to think so. Mom was in her first year of med school when she found out she was pregnant with me. My parents married and followed my father's sales job to Dallas. She never got to be a surgeon, but I like to think my successes are both of ours.

"So how do you like to spend your birthday, Gabe?" Tessa held up the lemon cupcake. "I assume it's more celebratory than cupcakes and tears."

"Movie night." Gabe winked. "An enormous pile of popcorn and a list of streaming titles."

"Well, that sounds lovely." Her eyes met his, and he saw a touch of the sadness give way to something different.

"Name the time and place, Tessa. I'll bring the popcorn." He grabbed the mint cupcake and dipped his finger into the icing.

Tessa's eyes widened, and she wagged a finger. "You're going to regret that!"

"Did you want the mint cupcake?" Gabe playfully started to offer his finger full of icing to her before remembering that *that* was more flirtatious than the night's conversation allowed. Trying to ignore the heat in his face, Gabe devoured the icing.

Tessa grabbed his hand. The warmth from the connection burned as she held him. *Does she feel it, too?*

Her eyes sparkled as she held his fingers up. "See!" She pointed to his bright green finger and laughed as Gabe felt his mouth slide open.

"How?"

Tessa continued giggling; her laughs made his green finger completely worth it. She wiped a happy tear from her cheek and held up the cupcake. "It's called the Minty Monster because they use so much food coloring in the icing that it stains anything it touches."

"The voice of experience?" Gabe leaned closer to her. Even with the tough conversations they'd had, the tears and green finger, there was no place Gabe would rather be tonight.

"The first time, my teeth were green for almost an entire day!" Tessa leaned closer, but still not near enough. Like they were magnets circling in an orbit, able to feel the pull of the other, but not close enough to get yanked together.

Yet.

"That cupcake is a kid and teenage favorite, so the bakery doesn't adjust the recipe. They make hundreds for Halloween. I always bring a dozen for the staff. The kids love our green mouths!"

She swallowed and met his gaze. "I really appreciate you coming tonight. It's been a long time since anyone noticed that I wasn't okay." She pushed a loose strand of hair behind her ear, and her gaze drifted to his lips just briefly. "And even longer since someone went out of their way to make me feel better."

"Any time." Gabe forced the words out. They

were true. But he was in danger of getting lost in the depths of her eyes again.

Before he could follow up, Tessa reached for his hand. "You said today that life was too short not to make everyone feel special. Is that why you came tonight...to make a friend feel special?"

The air crackled around them as he searched for the right words. In the end, the words refused to materialize. So he just let his heart talk.

"Life is too short not to do your best to make others realize that they matter." Gabe rubbed the delicate skin along her wrist, grateful when she didn't pull back. "But no. That's not why I showed up on your doorstep with five gourmet cupcakes and one green icing bomb!"

She bit her lip as she waited for him to continue.

"I wanted to check on you. I *needed* to make sure you were okay." Gabe rested his head against hers, measuring the subtle changes in her breath. "You matter to me. I have wished a thousand times that I'd called you after we were together. That I'd invited you to breakfast with my family that morning. That I'd told you how much I enjoy just being near you. I've spent the last week trying to figure out the best way to ask you to dinner."

"Wow." Tessa sighed as she moved around the

counter and slid next to him. "That was quite the pronouncement. I wish I'd called you, too. You matter to me, also."

His heart skipped a beat, not sure it could trust the statement. He wanted to pull her close, but there was a glint in her eye that stilled his hand.

"Can I ask you a question?" Tessa's voice was quiet as she crossed her arms.

Nerves raced around him, but Gabe nodded. "Anything."

"Did you not call because of my excitement over Dr. Lin's job?"

"Yes." Gabe let the truth rest between them. "And that wasn't fair to you. My mom left us like your father deserted you. Her career mattered more than her family. After our night together, seeing you dancing around the kitchen for a promotion made me nervous. And I'm sorry. That was wrong."

Tessa nodded, her lip twisting between her teeth. "I'm going for that position, Gabe." She pulled her arms tighter. "If that's a problem then we can just be friends. I won't hold it against you. I promise. But my ex demanded I refuse a similar position at a hospital in Ohio two years ago. I turned down that job for a man, and I won't do it again."

He blew out a breath as that truth sank between them. No wonder she hadn't called him!

But he wasn't going to make the same mistake as her ex-husband. "It's not a problem." Gabe pushed a curl behind her ear. "And it shouldn't have been a problem then. I panicked."

Tessa let her fingers lace through his. "Life at the hospital is hectic, and my schedule is…" She squinted as she looked for a word.

"Jam-packed?" Gabe offered.

"Yes." She nodded. "But I want to give this a try. Give us a try."

The air rushed from his lungs and Gabe couldn't remember the last time he'd smiled so much. His heart rang with joy as his brain echoed tiny warning bells, but they were easy to ignore when Tessa was touching him.

He should reach for this. He wanted to grab this! Life was too short to wait for happiness.

"Are you free Friday night?" Gabe ached to kiss her, to taste her again, but he sensed hesitation in Tessa, and he wouldn't rush this. If he was going to risk his heart again, then he wasn't going to give Tessa any reason to doubt him.

"No." Her bottom lip pushed out as she looked at him. "But I'm free Sunday. Have you ever been to the Dallas Botanical Garden?"

"Not since I was in high school." Gabe smiled. "But I'd love to see it this weekend."

"Then it's a date." Tessa beamed as she leaned

closer, her arms wrapped around his neck as she held him tight.

"Yes, it is," Gabe confirmed as he relished her body next to his. *Tessa.*

He ran a thumb along her cheek, grateful to get a second chance with this incredible woman.

When her lips met his, Gabe's body rejoiced. It wasn't the passionate need they'd experienced weeks ago. No, this kiss was comforting, and it spoke of tomorrow's promise.

It was perfect.

When she pulled back, he dropped a kiss along her cheek. "I'll see you at the hospital tomorrow."

Then he kissed the top of her head. "Happy birthday, Tessa."

CHAPTER SIX

"This place is bigger than I remember." Gabe's gaze wandered across the large parking lot.

Tessa bumped his hip with hers, enjoying the feel of his arm around her waist. They were on a date. Her heart felt like it might leap from her chest. She and Gabe were on a date.

"There are twenty-two gardens in all. At Christmas they set up twelve mock Victorian shops and houses to represent the twelve days of Christmas. The whole garden is sixty-six acres in total!" She bit back the other facts that wanted to pour from her lips.

This was one of her favorite places. She could recite as many facts as the volunteer tour guides who worked each of the gardens.

She'd wanted to be married here. But Max had balked at the notion. He wasn't going to contend with the garden's guests on their special day. Tessa had been hurt, but after her marriage had failed, she'd been grateful. At least she didn't have any poor memories here.

It felt right that she was here with Gabe. Tessa knew this was only their first date—their first real date, anyway—but she couldn't stop the smile spreading across her face as they crossed the threshold of the first garden.

"Sixty-six acres." Gabe squeezed her side as they wandered through the main entrance. "That's a lot of garden. So what other facts are popping around your brain, Tessa?"

"Am I that transparent?" She pulled him toward the Margaret Elizabeth Jonsson Color Garden.

"Transparent?" Gabe shook his head as he squeezed her waist. "You are basically bouncing. This is a place you have clearly been before—a lot, I'd wager."

Leaning her head against his shoulder, Tessa sighed as she drank in the peaceful settings. Even when the garden was full of families and picnic-goers, it always seemed like she was in her own bubble when she was here. Except now, Gabe was in her bubble, too. And that felt so right.

"I've been a member since I was a student in college. I used to come here to study on the grass yards. It's my happy place. Spring is my favorite. The tulips bloom for acres in the Color Garden. And you see everyone from brides-to-be, to girls celebrating their quinceañera, to moms and dads trying to snap the perfect picture of their rambling tots among the blossoms."

She used to dream of bringing her own small kids here. *But maybe...* Tessa pressed that bubble of hope away. This was their first date. It might feel like more because of their fiery first night, but she was not going to hope too much.

Clearing her throat, she pointed around the open space. "Right now it's got banana and tapioca plants in bloom. In a few weeks, it will be painted orange and purple with chrysanthemums."

"Really?" Gabe's gaze was focused on the field of colors before them.

Tessa swallowed the other plant information that was running through her brain. She'd had a thriving garden at the house she and Max sold. When she'd packed up her final things, she'd stood over the blooms she'd patiently coaxed from seedlings and cried. She'd driven by the house only once since her divorce and been horrified by the condition of her plants.

Except they weren't her plants anymore.

Her town house didn't really have the space for a large garden. She had a few ferns on her porch, but it wasn't the same. But she'd been doing some research on apartment gardens and she was pretty sure she could figure out a way to make a small green space happen.

"Sorry, I have a tendency to go overboard when talking plants." She pressed her free hand to her lips, willing all the things she wanted to say to stay buried.

"You don't need to apologize for being excited about something."

Gabe met her gaze and Tessa felt her spirit lift. It was such a small thing, to have someone willingly listen to her go on about the thing she enjoyed most. To care that she was excited.

"So, what's your favorite flower?"

"It's not here." Tessa leaned her head against his shoulder. Months ago, she'd come here on her own to see the tulips—and been painfully aware of how alone she was. This felt much more like an intimate day between long-term partners, and that should terrify her, but it was impossible to be worried when she was in her happy place... with Gabe.

"It's called Henry Duelberg salvia. It's drought-resistant and a deep bluish-purple. When you plant it in a bed, it will spread out, and—" Tessa watched Gabe's features shift. She always went overboard with plants. "Was that too much information?"

He chuckled and kissed her cheek. "Nope. But I was hunting for information on what types of blooms I might bring in the future that would make the smile you have right now appear."

"Oh." Tessa shook her head as they wandered towards the statues in A Woman's Garden. "I'm not sure there's a flower or plant you could bring me that wouldn't put a smile on my face. Though lantana does smell like gasoline if you brush against it, so maybe not that one."

Gabe pulled her into the shade and ran a hand along her cheek. "What if I leave it up to a florist to tell me which flowers will work, or maybe I'll grab some bundles at the grocery store? Those will look pretty enough on your table—at least until I learn the difference between lantana, salvia and roses, right?"

Learn the difference... Her eyes misted. She wasn't sure why she was so prone to waterworks these days, but she didn't care. She dropped a light kiss on his cheek. How had she gotten so lucky to be walking next to this man in her favorite place?

"Right," Tessa breathed out. But it wasn't Gabe's mention of a florist or his desire to make sure she had flowers that made joy race through her. It was his easy use of the word *future*. As though there would be more perfect moments like this to look forward to.

As a thrill rocketed through her, fear trickled behind it, too. Max had been interested early on, too. He'd never asked her favorite flower, but he'd been supportive of the garden she'd tended, helped her dig the beds and cooked dinner when she had to work late. She'd done her fair share, too, but when she'd gotten ahead, she'd asked him to take on a little more. And he'd hated her for it.

But as Gabe dropped his lips to hers, joy conquered fear—at least temporarily.

His touch was light, and Tessa craved more. Pulling him closer, she deepened the kiss. The gardens were lovely, romantic and the perfect place to kiss Gabe. Actually, the bar they'd reconnected in had felt perfect, too. She suspected every place might seem perfect when she was with him.

Gabe.

Her body molded to his as he stroked her back. "Aren't they cute?"

Gabe pulled back and Tessa felt her cheeks heat as she caught a few knowing looks from others walking past them. She'd smiled at many lovers who'd worn expressions of contentedness, too—but never been caught kissing in the gardens herself. It was a memory she knew she'd treasure.

Before she or Gabe could say anything, Tessa's phone buzzed. "Sorry." She pulled it out of her pocket.

"No, it's fine." His voice was breathless as he turned to look at the flowers.

Knowing that she could make the handsome, sweet, generous man beside her swoon made her euphoric. She quickly glanced at the text and typed out a reply.

"Everything okay?" Gabe's fingers were warm as they ran along her side.

Slipping her phone back in her pocket, Tessa grinned. "One of the residents ran into a case today that they had some questions on. They want me to look over their notes tomorrow and give them some feedback."

An emotion played across his face that sent a bead of worry pulsing through her. Many people took work calls on their off day. "I'm always available to help."

His lips twitched before Gabe nodded. "That's nice." He kissed her cheek as they started down the walking path. His eyes were far away, though his gaze was focused on the flowers in front of them.

Another twinge of uncertainty washed through her. Was he upset that so many people at the hospital relied on her? Had he not really meant it the other night when he said it shouldn't have mattered that she was so excited about the job opportunity? Max had done that—encouraged her to put in for promotions, then gotten upset when she got them.

No. Gabe was not Max. She would not let intrusive thoughts ruin this beautiful day and her time with Gabe.

She pointed out a few more of her beloved locations. Gabe nodded along and even asked questions. The disquiet that never quite left Tessa was silenced as they walked back to the car. Mostly.

"How did we manage to close the restaurant down?"

Tessa's laugh as they walked up to her town house door sent a thrill through him. After their day at the garden, Gabe had suggested they grab a quick dinner. *Quick.* He let out a soft chuckle, too.

"It really didn't feel like we'd been there for several hours." Gabe had made sure to leave the waiter a sizable tip for hogging the table for most of the evening. It had been unintentional, but he couldn't be sorry for it. Time just flew when he was with the woman beside him.

Tessa put her key in the door and turned the lock. Her dark eyes held his gaze as she leaned against the door. "I had the best time today, Gabe."

She leaned in, her soft kiss igniting flames

of need through his body. Her fingers ran along his stomach, and Gabe ached with desire. *Tessa.*

She pulled back and let out a breath. "I…" Tessa bit her lip. Her cheeks flamed. "I know our first night…"

Gabe dropped another kiss on her lips, then he smiled. If she invited him inside, he'd gladly carry her to bed and worship each inch of her again. But there was no need to rush anything. Gabe wanted Tessa for more than a one-night fling; he'd wait however long she needed to advance their relationship. "I'm in no rush, sweetheart."

He pushed a curl behind her ear, enjoying the heat of her skin beneath his fingers. He'd wait a lifetime for the woman in front of him, though he hoped it wouldn't be that long.

Tessa laid her head against his chest and sighed. "I had the best time today. The best."

Her repetition made his insides melt. *Best.* "I did, too, Tessa."

Wrapping his arms around her waist, Gabe kissed the top of her head, enjoying the feel of her against him. Then the top of her pants vibrated.

Another text message from the hospital?

During their date, she'd gotten at least ten messages or calls from interns and residents. Gabe had worked in the medical field for years and he understood that it was a calling to many. But Tessa was so tied to Dallas Children's.

No. He was not going to tumble down the path of worry. Tessa was helping, not trying to advance herself on the backs of others. And she didn't reach for the phone as he held her.

But Gabe couldn't hold her on her porch all night. No matter how much he might want to. Running his hand along the edge of her jaw, Gabe waited until she looked at him, then he dropped another kiss to her lips.

He didn't rush the kiss or deepen it. It was soft, and comforting, and full of the promise of more. So much more.

Pulling away, Gabe forced himself to take a step back, otherwise he might never make it off her stoop. "I can't wait to see you again, Tessa."

Her face lit with excitement. "I can't wait either, Gabe. Good night."

Tessa spun the scrambled eggs around on her plate and tried to calm the tumble of her stomach. She forced herself to take another bite. Protein was important, and she was just starting her shift, but her stomach twisted again. Maybe the extra dessert she and Gabe had ordered during their extended dinner last night had been a mistake.

She enjoyed sweets, but her body was not as

acclimated to the sugar as Gabe's. Electricity shot across her as she thought of him. Of their kisses on her porch.

Her body still ached with desire. Her dreams had all tumbled with images of him in her bed. Kisses and passion had lit through her sleep.

Until early this morning. After a peaceful night, she'd woken with a start from a nightmare. The remnants of the dream had faded quickly, but she remembered Gabe walking away from her after she received the promotion. It was just a product of an overactive subconscious. He'd said that he shouldn't have let the promotion keep him from asking her out. But the notch of uncertainty in the back of her mind refused to vanish.

The smell of the eggs made her queasy as she tossed her plate in the trash. Before she left the cafeteria, Tessa thought of grabbing a container of yogurt or a banana. But just looking at them made her stomach want to revolt. What was going on? Tessa rubbed her hand along her belly and started toward the nursing desk.

"Are you all right, Dr. Garcia?" Denise stared at her as Tessa reached for the thermometer.

Tessa's stomach lurched again, and she took a deep breath through her nose, trying to gather herself. "I'm not sure." She ran the thermometer along her forehead and sighed as it read ninety-eight point three. "No fever."

Her belly danced again, and she paged Dr. Killon. He was on call today. Even with no fever, she wouldn't be able to stay if her stomach was going to betray her. Most rotaviruses didn't present with a fever, but they were highly contagious—and often carried by children.

"Maybe my stomach just really wasn't in the mood for omelets today, but I've paged Dr. Killon." Her brain felt foggy as she uttered the words. Her overactive dreams must have kept her from truly resting—though she was not sorry to have spent the night dreaming of Gabe.

Denise nodded but kept her distance. The cleaning schedule at Dallas Children's was intense, but hospitals were breeding grounds for germs. "Shame, I love omelets. I ate them every Saturday until I was pregnant with Ginger. That little one hated eggs, though you'd never know it now!"

She grabbed a chart tablet. "I hope you feel better soon, Dr. Garcia."

"Thank you." Tessa barely forced the words through her lips as Denise's statement registered. *Pregnant...that is not possible.*

Except it might be. Tessa's nails dug into her palms as she calculated her last period. Two weeks before she and Gabe had been together. They'd used protection, but the condoms had been older, and protection wasn't perfect. She'd been busy, focused on the upcoming job opportunity, but how had she not noticed that she was so late?

She pressed her hands into her side as she felt her entire body start to shake. She needed to get out of here. Needed to gain control of herself—needed to stop by a pharmacy. What was she going to do?

One foot in front of the other. The mantra did little to calm her racing heartbeat as she started toward the employee lounge. If she was pregnant, she'd be almost eight weeks along. Over half-way through her first trimester. Her hands were clammy as she reached the lounge and pulled on her locker door.

Eight weeks along. That meant she'd spent most of her first trimester unaware of the little bean. She quickly racked her mind, trying to think through the last several weeks. She'd had alcohol the night she and Gabe... Her face heated at the memories.

Clearing her throat, she offered a short wave to a nurse as she headed for the parking garage. No alcohol since conception, but her caffeine habit had been maintained. Still, that wouldn't matter much at this early stage. And she hadn't been taking any prenatal vitamins.

Her chest tightened as she slid into the car. Prenatal vitamins were important, but many women started them after they discovered they were pregnant. The thought sent another wave of panic through her as she gripped her steering wheel. How was she calmly running through the checklist in her mind while her body was locked in terror?

She was probably overthinking this. In a few hours, she'd laugh at herself, order herself to look into stress relief tactics, and make an appointment with her gynecologist. It had been far too long since she'd seen Dr. Fillery anyway.

Her heart rocked a little at the idea that she might not be pregnant. She bit her lip as it started to tremble. That shouldn't make her upset—it shouldn't.

So why were tears coating her eyes?

Tessa forced air into her lungs as she tried to calm her aching heart. She'd wanted to be a mother for so long. To have a few little ones to come home to. But this wasn't the way she'd imagined it happening.

She and Gabe had decided to turn their one-night stand into something more. To see if the chemistry igniting them meant what they hoped. Yesterday had been so perfect, and Tessa was already looking forward to their next date.

How might an unplanned pregnancy change the mixture?

And Dr. Lin was filing his retirement paperwork next week—or maybe the week after that. Though all those rumors had been false so far.

She was not prepared for a baby. This was not the right time. But her heart didn't seem to care.

Tessa rolled her free hand over the still-flat portion of her lower belly. She knew it was far too early to feel anything—assuming she even was pregnant. But she was protective of the potential life growing inside her.

Her child.

She could do this.

Whatever this might be.

The tile floor in her bathroom was cold and hard, but she didn't feel like moving. Not yet. In the two hours it had taken her to buy a pregnancy test—four pregnancy tests, actually—Tessa had managed to convince herself that she'd been overreacting. But the double blue line on three of the tests did not lie.

She stared at the unopened fourth box. The urge to open it and confirm what the other three had stated was almost overwhelming. Rolling her head from side to side, she pushed back at that desire. The fourth test would only confirm what the second and third had.

Her life was changing. *And Gabe's life is changing, too.*

As if just her thoughts were enough to summon him, her phone buzzed.

You okay? Dr. Killon said you were sick.

Her fingers shook as she laid the phone aside. She should respond, should say she was fine. But was she?

Yes. No. Yes. The words spiraled through her mind as she pulled her knees to her chest. Laying her head against them, Tessa stared at her phone as another message popped in.

Let me know if you need anything.

It was such a sweet offer. The kind Gabe made—and meant—without even thinking. What was he going to do? If they'd known each other longer, today's revelations wouldn't cause her such worry.

Gabe was going to be an amazing father. Tessa swallowed. Assuming this was an adventure he wanted to take, too.

Wrapping her hands around her waist, Tessa tried to ignore the worry rooting its way through her mind. She didn't think Gabe would step away from her and their unexpected family. But her father had told her mother that he wanted a family when she'd discovered she was pregnant with Tessa. He'd promised to take care of them both, had professed a desire to be a family man. Then he'd abandoned them. And her ex-husband had discarded Tessa with little thought, too.

And she'd survived that, she reminded herself. She was strong, independent and caring, just like her mother. This wasn't the path to motherhood that she'd expected, but Tessa was going to show her child that they could do it all. No matter what.

Her child would never question that they were loved, wanted and treasured. Tessa laid her hands over the stillness of her belly and sighed. "I will always protect you."

At least she knew why she'd been such an emotional watering pot over the last few days. Taking a deep breath, Tessa tried to force her racing mind to focus. There were many things she needed to figure out. Things to do. Slapping her knees, she stood up.

Picking up her phone, she called her ob-gyn and walked to the kitchen. Pulling a glass down, she quickly swallowed her prenatal vitamin and started a small grocery list while she waited on hold. Then she texted Gabe and asked him to come over.

The text was vague; she didn't want to give

too much away. Particularly since Tessa hadn't figured out the right words yet. But this was not news that she wanted to relay over text or phone. He deserved to hear that he was going to be a father in person.

They were going to be parents.

Parents.

Gabe spun his phone around as he waited at the traffic light six blocks from Tessa's townhome. He was barely holding to his pledge to ignore his cellular device while in the car but he'd already memorized Tessa's cryptic texts. All four sentences.

We need to talk. Can you please come over after your shift?

He'd sent her a text back saying that he wasn't off until ten, but she'd responded to that, too.

I know. It's not something I want to put off.

Are you all right?

She'd read his last message three hours ago, according to his phone, and not responded. His hands were clammy as he gripped the steering wheel.

They'd had an excellent time at the gardens. The daytime date had spilled into a lovely evening. He'd thought it was perfect. Surely this wasn't a maybe-we-really-should-just-be-friends talk?

Could she really be having second thoughts?

Please, his soul whispered. He didn't want to give up on the possibilities his heart was painting.

He pulled into the small alley and tried to ignore the blood pounding in his ears and the tightness in his chest. What was waiting for him in Tessa's home? Gabe wiped his hands along the jeans he'd changed into after his shift, then forced himself to head to her back door.

The deck furniture where they'd sat so many weeks ago made him smile. That memory would always be good. *No matter what happened now.*

Her back door flung open, and Tessa stood in the bright light. Her shoulders were stiff, but he saw her fingers flex slightly. Something was bothering her. What had happened in less than twenty-four hours to make her so stressed?

"How are you feeling?" he asked as she stepped back to let him in. Denise had mentioned that Tessa's stomach had been upset, but Tessa looked all right now—at least physically.

A little tired, maybe. Her dark eyes met his. Worry floated across her gaze, but hope was there, too. That eased part of his concern, but only a little.

"I'm better now. Thanks for coming."

"Anytime." He hoped she knew how much he meant that. If she needed him, he'd be there for her. Gabe reached for her hand, and his heart loosened as she let him hold it.

"I'm pregnant."

The world shifted under his feet as Gabe tried to process the words. "Pregnant." His voice was barely above a whisper. "Pregnant?" He repeated. He should have said something else. Anything else, but the word just kept bouncing through his brain.

Tessa let go of his hand and moved toward the living room. "I'm sorry. I had an entire speech planned. I should have asked you to sit down." She sat on the end of the couch and drew her knees under herself as she motioned for him to sit on the other end.

She wanted him to take a seat, but not too close to her. Gabe tried not to let that sting. He was dealing with the news, but Tessa had only known for a few hours, too. Their lives were changing, but it would be okay.

He was going to be a dad. A sense of peace washed through him. *I'm going to be a dad.*

Excitement bubbled within him until he looked at Tessa's pale face. Was she not excited? This was a big change for him, but an even bigger one for her. What if she didn't want to be a mom?

Before he could let that concern take root, he let out a deep breath.

"You don't have to be involved." Tessa's voice was soft, but the words cut him. "I've worked everything out. I'll—we'll—be okay if this isn't something you want." Her fingers shook as she gripped her knees. "I know we've not discussed the future too much."

"I am not going anywhere, Tessa." Gabe was stunned as she let out a deep sigh. They'd only known each other a few weeks, but surely she knew him well enough to know that he wouldn't turn away from his child. *From her.*

Tessa nodded and pulled her knees even farther up—which he hadn't thought possible. "I know this wasn't planned. I don't want you to feel trapped. Our first *real* date was yesterday. I know we talked about another—"

"Do you not want another date? Because this news does not change that for me." Gabe slid next to her on the couch. She might not be ready to relax yet, but Gabe was here whenever she uncocooned herself.

Tessa looked at him, her eyes watering as she held his gaze. But the edge of a smile hovered on her lips.

"Are you okay? Denise said you looked positively green this morning."

"The baby doesn't like eggs." Tessa sent a small glare down to her belly, but it was followed by a brilliant smile. "Guess it's toast for right now."

"I bet the little bean will change his or her mind in a few years."

Tessa's bright grin sent a thrill through him.

"That's what I called the baby this morning. Little bean." She pulled her knees out from under herself but didn't slide any closer to Gabe. "I know I kind of sprang this on you. If you change your mind, I won't hold you to tonight's decisions. This certainly isn't how normal get-to-know-you dating starts."

Gabe couldn't argue with that, but he didn't care. He'd always wanted to be a father. This might not be the path he'd planned to walk, but he'd never turn his back on his child, or on Tessa. He hated the doubt he still saw floating in her expression.

"I won't change my mind, Tessa." Gabe laid his arm on the back of the couch, not touching her, but he hoped she viewed the open gesture as an invitation to move closer. "I've always wanted a family." It was the truth. He hadn't thought it was possible after he'd lost Olive, but staring at the woman across from him, Gabe couldn't be anything other than excited.

They were going to be parents. Parents!

He wanted, needed, her to know that he wasn't going anywhere. This was where he wanted to be. "I was stunned when you first told me. I'll admit I came over here fully expecting you to tell me we were not going to have another date, and I already reserved tickets for the holiday festival at the botanical gardens."

"You did?" Her mouth slipped into the small O shape that he'd found so enticing a few weeks ago. "That's months away. What if something goes wrong?"

His hand reached for hers, and his body relaxed as she let him hold it. He'd never tire of touching her. "Yes. It is months away. But I purchased them from my phone as soon as I got to my car last night. I'm banking on the future, Tessa. I want many dates between now and then, but I can't wait to see the Christmas village set up in a few months. Spending time with you is my favorite thing."

Tessa's bottom lip trembled as she slid next to him and put her head against his shoulder.

"Actually, I was wrong. This is my favorite thing. You in my arms."

Her eyes were bright as she looked up at him.

"This is my favorite thing, too. And the gardens are beautiful at Christmas. All the lights…"

His hand wrapped around her belly. Over the place where the child slept. They were going to be a family.

"I managed to get an appointment with Dr. Fillery tomorrow afternoon." Tessa looked up at him, and he saw her take a deep breath. "Her office had a last-minute cancellation. I know you're off tomorrow afternoon, too. Do you want to come?"

"Wild horses couldn't keep me away." Gabe sighed as she placed a light kiss on his cheek. Tonight was as close to perfection as he'd experienced in forever. "Want to try a movie night this weekend? See if the baby likes popcorn."

"That sounds lovely." Tessa closed her eyes, and her breathing slowed down as he held her.

"Then it's a date." Gabe kissed the top of her head and leaned his head back against the wall. Life had sent them a new twist, but it was going to be okay. Better than okay!

CHAPTER SEVEN

TESSA LET OUT a yawn and grinned. The smell of breakfast was one of the best things someone could wake to.

But she lived alone.

Her eyes flew open as she sat up. The room spun. Tessa held her head and groaned as her stomach lurched.

"Tessa?" Gabe's voice was strong but laced with worry as she felt him step beside her.

"Gabe?"

What time is it? What is he doing here? Will breakfast taste as good as it smells?

A piece of bread was pressed into her palm.

What is going on?

"Try a couple small bites. Stacy swore by a slice of toast first thing in the morning to curb some of her morning sickness."

Tessa took a bite out of the corner, then looked up. He was really here. "You didn't leave?" He hadn't left after she'd fallen asleep. Had he held her all night long?

They'd slept together again—except this time it had been on her couch. Nothing physical had happened between them, so why did this action feel so much more intimate? So much more permanent?

"I was surprised when I woke up, too." Gabe's lips turned up as he sat beside her. "Not sure how we slept so soundly on your couch, but I guess we were both past the point of exhaustion." His hand lay across her knee. The warmth it carried calmed her as much as the toast.

She let her gaze linger on his hand for a minute. So many things were running through her mind as she finished the piece of toast. He was right; her stomach felt infinitely more secure.

"I should have asked before I went rummaging through the kitchen, but you were still asleep. You barely noticed when I slipped away." He pulled on the back of his neck as he met her gaze. "And with the morning sickness yesterday, I figured—" He looked at her as his words died away.

She kissed his cheek, enjoying the fact that he'd stayed more than she probably should. "You figured you'd help." Tessa smiled.

"It's the thing I do best. Gotta earn my keep." Gabe offered a silly salute. "Do you want some ham? I fried up some in case your stomach was ready for something besides toast."

"Thanks," Tessa answered as she stood. Gabe was next to her, not touching but close.

Was he staying close in case she got dizzy again?

The gesture was sweet, but Tessa felt a touch of worry. They were going to be parents, but she didn't need him to watch her every step. Pregnancy wasn't a disease; it was something women had been doing since before the written word.

"It's nice that you like helping." She leaned against him, enjoying Gabe's strength. It balanced her before she started for the kitchen. She waved him away from the cupboard as she grabbed a few plates. She could fix her own breakfast plate.

"I'm the oldest, remember? I learned early on how to earn my keep in my large family." His eyes were bright as he watched her grab her breakfast before fixing his own. "Even before my mother walked out, I was more of a third parent to Isla. I swear she's been getting into trouble since the moment she was born."

He let his gaze wander to her belly, and Tessa's cheeks heated. He was happy about this... he really was.

"Isla is going to be thrilled to be an aunt again. She loves to dote on little ones."

She could see the pride radiating off him.

Their child would have cousins and aunts and uncles to watch them. A built-in extended family.

But what would *her* place be? She'd let herself be absorbed into Max's friendship group. And when the marriage failed, she'd been pushed out. She and Gabe would always be connected by their little one, but if they didn't work out…

Why was she plotting the worst-case scenario?

Because that was what always happened. Her heart ached at that truth. Just because her father had left her mother and Max had walked away, that didn't mean that her relationship with Gabe was doomed.

Particularly if she made sure that he never felt put upon like Max had.

"Coffee?" Gabe offered as he rummaged through her cabinet.

"I can do that." Tessa got off the stool.

"Just point me in the direction of the coffee filters. It's no big deal."

"What?"

Tessa's blood iced at Gabe's statement. It was the line Max had thrown around constantly when she'd asked him for help. *It's no big deal* had been the phrase she'd learned meant he was in a foul mood, resenting that she'd asked him for help.

"I said point me toward the coffee filters. Oh,

never mind!" Gabe spun around holding the stack.

He laid a cup of coffee in front of her.

"Are you okay?" Gabe's gaze hovered on her. His eyes shone with worry.

"Does the little bean not like ham?" Worry lines pressed into the corners of his eyes as he started toward her.

"No." Tessa's voice was stronger than she'd expected. "I just don't gobble up my breakfast." She smiled, hoping it covered the anxiety coursing through her.

He playfully threw a hand across his chest.

The feigning-hurt gesture almost fully lifted her spirits.

"What time is the appointment this afternoon? Think they'll let us see the little one?"

"I hope so." Tessa grinned. She'd love to see the baby. And she couldn't wait to see Gabe's reaction to their child. He was going to love seeing the dancing bean.

At eight weeks there wouldn't be much definition, but she smiled knowing they might get a glimpse of their little one.

She stood and scooped the last bite of ham into her mouth before starting toward the sink.

"I can get that." Gabe held out his hand, waiting for her plate.

"It's fine, Gabe. I can do it." The worry lines

reappeared, but he stepped away. She wasn't going to let him do everything for her. No matter how nice it might feel. She was pregnant, but that didn't mean that she needed help.

And she wouldn't risk his future resentment.

"My appointment is at three at the Plano office. Only the nurse practitioner works in the Dallas office on Tuesday, and I didn't want to wait." Tessa dried the plate and put it back in the cupboard.

"Do you want me to pick you up? I need to at least swing by Stacy's to shower and change clothes." His face brightened as he mentioned his sister.

"I have a few errands beforehand. I'll just head to the doctor from there."

"I don't mind running errands." Gabe smiled.

She wanted to say yes. To ask him to come along. But she was only going to look at maternity clothes. It was still too early for her to need much, but with her hectic schedule, it would be good to have a few things on hand while she had a chance. But picking out stretchy pants was only going to be interesting or fun for her.

Her ex-husband had grumbled even when she'd wanted to make a quick stop, and Tessa suspected this wouldn't be a swift outing. No, she was going to enjoy each moment of this experience. This was an avenue where she could spare Gabe.

His gaze raked across her, but Gabe didn't press. "I'll see you at Dr. Fillery's at two fifty, then."

"Two forty." Her throat was tight as she explained, "I have to be there at two forty to fill out paperwork." She could fill out documents without him, but she didn't tell him that. It was a little thing, but she wanted him there when she walked into the office.

"Then I'll see you at two forty." He stepped next to her, his gaze holding her steady.

Her mind was racing with a million different excitements and more than a few worries, but as she slipped into his arms, her body quieted.

She wrapped her arms around his neck and kissed him, sighing as he pulled her tight. So much had changed over the last few weeks, but her body still reacted to Gabe the same. Still seemed to call out with joy and need as he touched her.

As he walked out, she hugged herself. Suddenly two forty seemed very far away.

Gabe hustled down the stairs of the parking garage. He hadn't expected there to be so much traffic between his sister's place and Plano. He'd been back in the Dallas area for over six months, but he still hadn't gotten used to the increased traffic. Normally, he gave himself extra time to get anywhere, but getting out of his sister's house had been a trial.

Stacy had peppered him with questions when he'd arrived home. She'd wanted to know all about the woman he'd spent the night with twice. And whether they were dating. He understood Stacy's questions and the concern he saw hovering in her eyes—to a point. She didn't want to see him hurt.

But there'd been no way to explain where he was going this afternoon without also saying he was going to be a father. And that conversation would have resulted in his phone blowing up with calls and texts. Secrets were not a thing in the Davis family.

He wasn't quite ready to subject Tessa to that. The Davis clan would love her and gladly initiate her into their crazy brood. But the Davis family was so many things.

Loud, intrusive and loving beyond measure. Overwhelming didn't begin to describe his family.

Tessa would fit in perfectly.

She was a strong, independent woman. But that didn't mean that she didn't need someone to care about her. He wanted to make things easier, particularly now that she was pregnant.

But that urge had been there before he'd found out about their impending bundle. Tessa made him happy. It was as simple—and as complicated—as that.

But what if she didn't want his help?

The worry tickled the back of his brain. That was the thing Gabe did best. He thrived on making sure those he cared about knew they could always ask him for anything. But Tessa had seemed unsettled by it this morning.

He tried to remind himself that she hadn't had someone to look after her. Maybe she just wasn't used to it. But the worry still bounced around his brain as he shuffled around a car in the parking garage.

Tessa could handle anything—Gabe would never doubt that—but it didn't mean she needed to shoulder all the burdens that were coming.

He was an expert at lightening the load. He'd just have to figure out a way to show her that she could rely on him for anything. *Always.*

"You still have a few minutes," Tessa's voice carried across the parking garage.

He spun and felt the small bead of warmth that had nothing to do with the afternoon heat spread through him as she started toward him.

She stepped next to him and hesitated only a minute before sliding her hand into his. "You ready for this?"

"I think so." Gabe matched her stride as they entered the building with at least a dozen different doctor's offices. The blast of air-conditioning sent a shiver through him, and he was glad that Tessa led the way. "I'm a little nervous."

"Me, too. This isn't the exact path I saw myself on to becoming a mom." Tessa's free hand rested over her belly. "But it's exciting." She let out a nervous laugh. "Everything is topsy-turvy, terrifying, happy, and I feel like I'm grasping at marbles as they all drop around me."

Squeezing her hand, he opened the office door she stopped in front of. "I think that's almost everyone's description of having a baby."

Tessa kissed his cheek. "I'm so glad you're here."

His heart sang as he followed her. *Here we go!*

Tessa's vitals were fine, and the nurse asked her the basic questions as Gabe hung to the side. Even though they were both medical professionals, he could see the bit of worry tracing across Tessa as she looked at the heartbeat monitor and gel on the counter. He'd glanced at them several times, too.

It was important for the nurse to get all the details, but waiting to hear the heartbeat was growing harder with each passing second. She was nearing her eighth week. The first trimester was always the riskiest for miscarriage. He knew that as many as 20 percent of known pregnancies ended in miscarriage. They were devastatingly common, which made the relative silence around them sadder.

But the metric also meant that nearly many pregnancies made it to delivery. At seven weeks, almost eight, their child's heartbeat should be strong and bright. But until they heard it, they'd each wonder—and worry.

"Can you lean back for me? This may be cool." The nurse smiled as Tessa lay back.

Gabe leaned closer, his eyes moving from Tessa's face to where their baby was growing. Her belly still betrayed no sign of their impending joy. When Tessa reached for his hand, he grabbed hers and squeezed. The nurse rolled the heartbeat monitor over Tessa's lower abdomen, and they each let out a sigh as a strong beat echoed through the monitor. Then the beat adjusted. The nurse's nose scrunched, and her forehead tightened for just a moment as she lifted the heartbeat monitor. She hid her reaction, but not quick enough.

Tessa's fingers clenched at her sides.

"What is it?" Gabe asked as the nurse lifted the monitor.

The nurse didn't glance at him as she asked Tessa, "How far along did you say you were?"

"Seven weeks—almost eight." Tessa's voice was tight as she stared at the nurse.

"Great." She tapped Tessa's hand. "Dr. Fillery will be in shortly."

It took all Gabe's restraint to keep his seat and not beg her to roll the heartbeat monitor back over Tessa's belly so he could try to catch what she had. As a nurse, he knew that it was the doctor's responsibility to pass along diagnoses, but he also knew that he often knew exactly what was wrong with a child, too. You didn't work in a specialized area without picking up the most common diagnosis capability—and even some less common ones.

He also knew from the look on the nurse's face as she patted Tessa's hand that she wouldn't tell them what was going on. That was the correct procedure, but when it was your baby, the emotions swirling around you felt so different.

He'd learned after losing Olive that life sometimes didn't let you protect those you loved. But Gabe would do everything in his power to protect Tessa and their child. *Anything.*

As soon as the door closed, Tessa's scared gaze met his. "Did you hear whatever made her demeanor shift?"

"No." Gabe shook his head and moved to her side. Her fingers tightened in his as he squeezed his eyes shut and tried to think through what he'd heard. "I was so focused on the happy sound. The heartbeat sounded strong. Fast—but that's normal at this stage." He knew Tessa knew that, but he was just trying to figure out anything.

"When she rolled it closer to my belly button, it sounded a little slower. But that shouldn't matter. Should it?"

His top knuckle cracked as Tessa squeezed his hand even tighter.

"Sorry." She released him.

Gabe pulled her hand back. "Nothing to apologize for. That's just the result of me cracking my knuckles since I was ten." Lifting her fingers to his lips, Gabe placed a light kiss on her hand. "No matter what, I'm here for you. Okay?"

She nodded her head and stared at the door. "You never realize how long this feels from the other side—huh! We run from patient to patient—usually skipping meal breaks and living on caffeine. But now I want to run out that door and scream for Dr. Fillery to march in here."

Gabe chuckled as Tessa laid her free hand against her forehead. "I'm itching to rip the door open myself. But we are going to be patient, right?"

"I guess." Tessa laid a hand across her belly. "I'm just a ball of nerves."

"A gorgeous ball of nerves." Gabe kissed her

fingers again, and a bit of the tension leaked from him. He loved touching Tessa, loved the feel of being near her. No matter what Dr. Fillery came in to discuss, Gabe knew they could handle it. Maybe that was naive given how long they'd known each other, but Gabe couldn't imagine it going any other way. He and Tessa were meant to be in each other's lives. They just were.

He wasn't sure where that certainty came from. But as she met his gaze, warmth burst through him again. She was his second chance. Gabe swallowed as that thought, that knowledge, settled around him.

The door opened and they both straightened. He'd have to work out exactly what that meant some other time.

"What did your nurse hear?" Tessa rushed the words out. "Sorry, she told me her name, but I'm panicking and can't recall."

Dr. Fillery offered a smile as she pulled the portable ultrasound machine toward Tessa. "Meghan thinks she heard two heartbeats."

"Two!" The word flew from Gabe's lips and heat flooded his body as Tessa looked from him to the ultrasound machine. "Sorry."

"It's fine," Dr. Fillery stated. "It may have just been that she caught the baby's heart rate shifting." She dropped more gel on Tessa's abdomen, then picked up the ultrasound wand. "Let's take a look."

Gabe doubted that the nurse had just heard the heartbeat shifting. He couldn't imagine a nurse working in obstetrics and not being able to identify multiple babies' heart rates. It would be like Gabe hesitating to differentiate between the chicken pox, rubella and measles rash. You just knew—even if the doctor passed along the actual notes and follow-up.

It took only a few seconds for the wand to find the sac. Gabe swallowed as he stared at the images on the screen. Two babies in one amniotic sac—identical twins. He was going to be a father...to two!

CHAPTER EIGHT

TWINS! TESSA'S FEET pounded on the tile of her kitchen floor. She hadn't stopped moving since she and Gabe had left the doctor's office.

She was pregnant with twins. *Identical twins.* All multiples carried risks, but identical twins were more likely to be born early and more likely to need the NICU. More likely to result in bed rest for the mother.

Her chest seized. She laid a hand across her belly; the babies were safe right now, and she needed to focus on that. Tessa squeezed her eyes shut and tried to force all the racing thoughts from her mind.

But they refused to vacate the premises.

How was she supposed to raise two at once? Her heart pressed against her chest. Tessa pushed a hand through her curls as she tried to rework everything she'd started.

She'd measured the room she was using as an office this afternoon. Two cribs could fit in there, but it would be tight. And she'd window-shopped for a crib, a high chair and clothes while grabbing a few maternity items, but she'd focused on the safety ratings, not the cost of outfitting two at once. The day care bills alone…

Her chest tightened again. She was not going to panic. At least not any more than she already was.

And the promotion? Her skin prickled as she tried to remember the meditation tricks she'd learned during her residency. *Breathe…clear your mind.*

Would the human resources department even consider her a candidate now?

That thought wasn't helpful, but it refused to cede its place in her brain. Technically, it wasn't legal for them to discard her résumé due to pregnancy, but there would be no way to prove it.

No. She could be a twin mom and a senior attending in the emergency room. Her maternity leave might be longer than with a single pregnancy, and the possibility of bed rest was higher. The blood pounded in her ears, and Tessa ran her hands along her arms.

Breathe.

She'd just have to double her efforts at the hospital while she could. Her mother had lost her chance for the career she wanted because of an unplanned pregnancy. But it had been a different time, and they hadn't been able to afford day care and med school.

If she hadn't acquiesced to Max's demands, she'd already be a senior attending.

But then you wouldn't have met Gabe. Wouldn't be carrying twins. Wouldn't have this incredible chance at a family.

She couldn't wish that she was in Cincinnati now.

Tessa stroked her belly where two children— *her* children—were currently growing. She was going to take care of them. She could do this. All of it.

"Tessa." Gabe's voice sounded far away. His hand was warm as he grabbed her, and her heart slowed its racing pace. His anchor stabilized her.

"We need to figure this out." Tessa's voice was ragged as she stared at him. "How are you so calm?"

"That isn't an adjective I'd use to describe myself right now. But I'm trying to think of it as an adventure." His fingers brushed her cheek before he leaned his head against hers. "With double the diapers!"

She laughed. It felt good to release some tension. His rich scent sent a wave of solace through her. "I love how you smell." The compliment slipped from her lips. She knew that pregnancy heightened the senses, but it seemed like such a silly thing to say when they were trying to determine a path forward.

"That's good to know." Gabe pressed a kiss to her forehead. "I know there's a lot to do. And it seems scary, but can we focus on the positives for a second?"

"The positives?" Tessa raised an eyebrow. They'd gone from a one-night stand to parents-to-be, to parents-of-twins-to-be, before they'd even made it to a second date. The things that needed to be done looked more like mountains than minor to-do lists. But as Gabe held her, the panic that had been on a near-constant rise abated.

"You're healthy and our children are also healthy. Those two things mean everything." Gabe smiled, his dimples popping.

She hoped the babies inherited those!

She saw his gaze shift down her body. Tessa squeezed his hand. Then she laid it over the place where their children were growing.

He dropped a light kiss to her lips. "It's going to be okay. Our hands may be full, but we can do this—together. Promise."

His hand sent sparks along her skin, even through the light gray shirt she wore today. The connection between them crackled as it had since that first night. He seemed so certain, so sure that it was going to be all right. So sure that they had a future. Why couldn't she focus on that possibility? Maybe everything would work out for her—*finally*.

"So, what do we do first?" Tessa turned to grab a glass of water; she was still a little too keyed up to stay in one place.

"Well, we probably need to alert Human Resources."

"No." Tessa shook her head. "Dr. Lin's position is opening." She was so close to fulfilling her dream. To earning what her mother's unplanned pregnancy had stolen from her. Another chance might not open for several years. At least not at Dallas Children's. And she doubted Gabe would want to move. He was more tied to this area than Max was. Now was her best shot.

"Tessa." Gabe closed his eyes. His lips pursed.

He was frustrated—with her. A shiver of worry pressed against her spine. She wanted to keep this to themselves, at least for a few more weeks, but she hated upsetting Gabe.

She'd watched Max pull away from her whenever he was upset with her. Tessa had learned to control her emotions around her ex. But with pregnancy hormones racing through her, it was harder then ever.

Gabe hadn't reacted poorly to her tears when he'd brought over cupcakes. Hadn't gotten angry at the fear and panic she was displaying or told her to get a hold of herself. He seemed genuinely happy to help.

Maybe relying on him for something wouldn't lead to disaster? Surely he wouldn't blame you for his unhappiness? She felt her eyes widen at that thought. Gabe's eyes shifted, too—the man noticed everything.

"Tessa," Gabe's voice broke as he pulled her to him.

Before he could get any further, she offered, "I'm not through my first trimester. Dr. Fillery said everything was fine, but it's still early. I promise to alert Human Resources when I enter my second trimester."

Maybe by then a decision would have been made about Dr. Lin. She hated the thought. But she owed her mom. And she wanted to be a senior attending.

He pulled back a little and wiped a stray tear from her cheek. He smiled, "Okay. No telling HR until the second trimester."

He dropped a chaste kiss to her lips. "What if you help me look for an apartment? I can't really have the twins over to my sister's place when they're with me. Her couch was getting uncomfortable, anyway."

His statement struck her. *With him.* Tessa hadn't considered that her children would have two homes. The idea of her children being somewhere else brought tears to her eyes—again. *Hormones!*

It was ridiculous. Many people shared custody, but Tessa didn't want that—at least not when they were first born. "What if you moved in here?"

The question shot out, and there was no way to reel it back. Her heart rejoiced while her brain screamed. She had plenty of room in her town house. And the idea didn't seem so preposterous as she met Gabe's gaze.

She was on dangerous ground. It would be so easy to fall for him. *Fall for him more.*

But Tessa couldn't bring herself to retract the offer. Instead, she crossed her arms and dug in further. "I just mean, I have a spare bedroom. I was going to put the baby—babies," she corrected, "in the study since I never really use it. I want to breastfeed for at least the first few months, so they'd need to be here, anyway." The more she talked, the more this made sense.

And if he was willing to give the future a shot, she could, too.

"I know it's an unorthodox arrangement but…"

Tessa threw her hands in the air. She didn't want Gabe locked into a yearlong lease somewhere else. Didn't want her children split between homes from the second they were born. And she wanted Gabe close.

That was terrifying. But having him somewhere else made her heart ache more. Her palms were clammy as she waited for his answer.

"Why start with the traditional now? Whatever traditional means?" Gabe shrugged. "Are you sure, Tessa? If you want to take a few days to think it over…"

She didn't want to think it through. Gabe belonged here with their children. With her.

"No. I don't need a few days. We're a family now. Maybe an unusual one. But a family."

Family.

The word wrapped around her as she let Gabe pull her close again. Her heartbeat stabilized as she breathed in his scent. How long had it been since she'd belonged to a family? *A real one.* Not since the early days of her marriage to Max. As soon as he'd failed to advance at work, she'd become a competitor instead of his wife. An interloper in her own marriage.

But Gabe would never make her choose between her career and their relationship. He'd promised her.

"Family." Gabe brushed his lips against hers. Maybe this wasn't the usual path, the safe one, but for the first time in forever, Tessa's felt like her feet were on secure ground.

"We have one other thing we need to do."

Gabe's grin was bright, but she thought she saw him hesitate a little.

He was always so sure of himself. The hesitation stunned her. "What?" Tessa put her hand on his chest and was surprised that it was thrumming. What was he so nervous about?

"We have to tell the Davis clan."

Tessa swallowed as she met his gaze. "Name a time and place." Then she raised her lips to his. Her life had shifted completely. But when she was with Gabe, those changes no longer seemed so frightening—in fact, they seemed perfect.

The alarm had gone off far too early for Tessa. Particularly now that she couldn't dose herself with a giant pot of caffeine fifteen minutes after her feet hit the ground. And waking alone no longer brought her any comfort either. Had it ever?

She didn't investigate that thought as she smiled at Gabe before he ducked into a patient's room. Gabe's family was helping him move in this weekend. He swore that it wouldn't take long. Apparently, even the stuff he'd moved into storage the first weeks he'd been here had only been a bedroom suite and a beat-up couch that he suggested they drop at the curb. The rental unit was close to Southern Methodist University. Gabe was confident that the battered but not broken piece would find a home in a college apartment.

"He *is* something!" Denise's statement broke through Tessa's mental wanderings as she handed her a tablet chart. "I know Gina and Rochelle are hoping that he might ask them out. I told them not to get their hopes up."

"You did?" Tessa tried to pretend that it wasn't jealousy racing up her spine. Gabe was kind, well-educated and stunning. Of course the single staff would be interested in him.

She winked at Tessa before leaning closer. "He only has eyes for you."

Tessa's cheeks heated as Denise leaned away. "Oh. Well. We're—" Her voice faltered as she tried to find the right words.

They were going to be parents and were moving in together, but they'd agreed it was too early to share a bedroom.

He promised they could move as slow or as fast as she wanted on this path they were traveling together. But that didn't leave a lot of standard definition for Tessa to fall back on in this situation.

"Don't worry." Denise grabbed another tablet chart. "Whatever it is, your secret is safe with me."

"Thank you." Tessa nodded. "I'll see to the little guy in room three."

"I know he's here for a stomach issue. But the little sister may have fifth disease." Denise swiped up on the chart she had in her hand and didn't catch the panic rippling through Tessa. "They noticed it in triage."

Fifth disease, also called erythema infectiosum, was a common childhood illness. Most kids had a low-grade fever and cold before a bright red rash spread across their cheeks, and occasionally their bodies. It was almost always mild. Except in pregnant women.

Her hands itched to stray to her belly, but they weren't discussing her pregnancy at the hospital. Fifth disease was most dangerous in the first half of pregnancy.

She'd likely had fifth disease, but she didn't know for sure. And it was nearly always asymptomatic in adults. Unless you miscarried. Tessa took a deep breath. She hadn't told anyone about her pregnancy, and the little boy had been ill for several days. She had to walk into the room. She'd take all the viral precautions she could.

"Hi." Tessa smiled through her fear as she stepped into the room. The small boy on the bed was lying on his side, holding his tummy. He looked miserable. The child's father was holding his little sister. Her cheeks were bright red, and he looked exhausted, too.

The door to the room opened, and Gabe

stepped in. "Denise said you might need a hand." His nose scrunched as he met Tessa's gaze. She glanced toward the sister and saw Gabe follow her gaze.

"Hey, cutie."

Gabe bent to examine the sister while Tessa turned her attention to the little one on the table. "Can you tell me what's going on?"

The boy's eyes teared up, but he didn't say anything.

Tessa looked toward his father. "What can you tell me?"

The father looked from Tessa to Gabe, and she saw his shoulders sag even further as he looked at his child. "I don't know much. Ryan can't seem to keep food in. He doesn't throw up, but he's been in the bathroom for days. I've been working extra shifts this month." His voice wavered.

"My wife—ex-wife—might know, but she isn't returning my calls. She…" He let his words drift away.

"Okay." Tessa saw the desperation in the father's face. Heard it as he looked between his two kids. Her mother had worn the same expression in many of the memories Tessa could dredge from her mind. "What did you eat last?"

She moved to the sink and washed her hands as Ryan rubbed a tear from his cheek.

"Mac and cheese. It tasted good, but my belly

hurt after. Now it feels like someone is jabbing it with knives. It's never been this bad before." Ryan clenched his teeth as he gripped his belly.

So Ryan had been experiencing the issues for a while. "Does it hurt if you eat bread?" Tessa asked as she caught Gabe's gaze.

He held up a five as he headed for the sink, too. So he thought that Ryan's little sister had fifth disease, too. Nurses might not make official diagnoses, but every pediatric nurse could identify the different common childhood rashes. She'd double-check the rash, but if two of her nurses thought the rash looked like fifth disease, then she'd be shocked if it wasn't.

That was a worry for another hour.

Right now, Tessa was concerned that Ryan had celiac disease, or one of the other autoimmune diseases that attacked the intestinal tract.

"I don't eat bread. It makes me—" The boy's cheeks turned bright red.

"Fart?" Gabe smiled as he winked at the boy.

Ryan nodded but didn't say anything else. Most boys this age enjoyed talking about bodily functions. In fact, Tessa had participated in more conversations regarding gas with boys between the age of six and twelve than she had ever thought possible when she graduated from medical school.

If you were dealing with painful gas all the

time, it could go from something silly to giggle about with friends to something you were embarrassed about really quickly. Unfortunately, there was no quick diagnosis for celiac disease. It would take a few weeks to confirm. But if they were right, then shifting his diet could bring him some instant relief.

"I think Ryan may have celiac disease. It means his body cannot process gluten. While he's here, I'm going to order a blood work panel. We'll also need to rule out a parasitic infection."

Moving around the table, Tessa squatted in front of Ryan's little sister. "Hi, sweetheart." The little girl buried her head in her dad's chest, but she'd seen enough. Her cheeks looked like they'd been slapped, and there was a rash on her arms. Classic fifth disease presentation.

She met the exhausted father's gaze, "And your daughter has the symptoms of fifth disease."

Ryan's father blinked as his gaze shifted from his son to his daughter. "What?"

"The runny nose, pink cheeks and the rash on her arms." Tessa nodded. "The good news is that there really isn't anything to do for that except treat any symptoms if she gets uncomfortable."

"I am really failing at this single-parent thing, guys." Ryan's father kissed the top of his daughter's head.

"It's okay, Daddy." His daughter looked at him, her eyes so full of love that Tessa's heart nearly broke.

"Yes, it is," Tessa reiterated. "I need to talk to your dad real quick. But Nurse Gabe is going to stay with you guys."

"Yep." Gabe made a mock salute that caused Ryan and his little sister to grin.

The hallway was quiet as she stepped into it.

"I know I messed up," Ryan's dad started, and Tessa held up her hand.

"You didn't. You brought your son to the hospital, and kids get fifth disease all the time—literally! What's your name?"

"Adrian Farns." He wrapped his arms around himself and looked at the closed door where Gabe was probably starting to draw Ryan's blood for the autoimmune panel workup.

"I didn't bring you out here to discuss poor parenting. Negligent parents don't worry about their kids or bring them to the ER unless it's critical. You *are* doing a good job." Tessa offered what she hoped was a bright and comforting smile. "I wanted you to know that what your children need most is you."

Adrian blinked. "What?"

"You're exhausted, Adrian. That is a natural state for most parents, I know. But I think your exhaustion goes deeper."

His shoulders sagged even further. How heavy the weight of the world must seem to the man before her. "I came home to a note about four months ago. My wife—ex-wife—had left the kids with the neighbor, cleaned out the bank account and run off with her boyfriend. It's been a lot to handle."

"I bet." Tessa nodded. "I'm going to give you a list of dietary restrictions and recipes to try with Ryan to get him some relief. But I'm also going to include a list of services that can support your family through this. All the worldly goods don't matter if you're not there."

During her first year at Dallas Children's, she'd worked with their social worker to put together a solid list of contacts for services that could help parents. Whether they were struggling with financial issues, mental health issues or grief, Dallas Children's had a printout. The social worker made sure that the list of contacts was regularly updated.

If Tessa's mother had known who to ask for help, she might be celebrating becoming a grandparent now. She'd give as many people as possible the opportunities her family hadn't gotten.

Adrian nodded. "Thank you."

"You're welcome. Someone will be in with all those papers in a little while. If Ryan gets dehydrated, please bring him back. And introduce new foods slowly. His digestive system is at war."

Adrian mumbled a few words before heading back into the room with his kids. And Tessa headed toward the employee bathroom to scrub off the room's germs.

Tessa's hands were red by the time Gabe found her. He knew the odds of fifth disease transmission were minuscule. But in the 1 to 3 percent of pregnancies it affected, the consequences were catastrophic. And those numbers didn't seem so tiny when it was your children.

"I don't think any germs could have survived that scrubbing, Tessa." Gabe tried to keep his voice light as he reached for the taps and turned off the water. He hoped she hadn't burned her skin. Even if she hadn't, the vicious cleaning was going to leave them sore. Gabe made a mental note to make sure they had aloe vera or some other cooling lotion at home.

She held up her wrinkled digits and swallowed. "We have to tell Human Resources."

Gabe was stunned by the reaction. After her vehement refusal last night, he'd expected to argue the point with her. To have to address why they needed to be open about this.

When his mother had been pregnant with Isla, she'd been put on bed rest toward the end. Some of the worst fights between his parents had occurred during that period. His mother had been determined not to lose her position at the marketing firm where she worked. She'd only taken time off when the doctor had told her if she went into labor again, she'd have to be hospitalized until delivery.

There was no need to get into the actual details with everyone, but for Tessa's and the twins' safety, they needed to keep her from highly infectious rooms. There were only a handful of diseases that Tessa wouldn't be able to treat anyway. It was standard protocol for pregnant medical staff. She wasn't asking for any special treatment.

There would be some whispers, but at least a few of their colleagues already suspected that they were seeing each other. And hospital gossip shifted to new topics with lightning speed.

"I'm up-to-date on all my vaccinations. It should have a minor impact." Tessa voiced the thoughts that were rattling around in Gabe's mind. "And I'll let Patrick know that this will have no impact on my decision to apply for Dr. Lin's position."

And we're back to the promotion.

"Sure." His voice was more clipped than he'd meant it to be, but Tessa didn't seem to notice. Gabe understood wanting to advance at work.

He understood Tessa's drive to be successful. But she was already incredibly successful.

What if, after this promotion, there was another and another? He'd watched medical professionals chase glory during his career. Higher pay and more prestige always came with trade-offs. And they were usually borne by the families.

Was that what Tessa wanted?

No, Gabe forced the thought to the back of his brain. If that was all Tessa wanted, he'd have already seen it by now. She loved their little ones, even though they were barely bigger than a cherry.

She'd scrubbed her skin raw out of fear of a disease that she'd almost certainly been exposed to dozens of times as a pediatric physician—even if she hadn't had it as a child. He'd heard her telling Ryan's father that he needed to take care of himself, too. And Gabe had seen the papers outlining how to deal with parental stress and divorce in the discharge notes he'd pulled up for Ryan. Those were not the actions of a woman who would put her work before everyone else.

Gripping her hands, Gabe wanted to make her smile. To lighten the day's heavy mood. "So, since we are having identical twins, there is one serious issue we need to consider." He tapped the edge of her nose as her eyes widened. "How do we keep from mixing them up?"

"What?" Tessa laughed.

The sound sent joy ping-ponging around his soul. Her smile lit up the room and his life. He'd do anything to make that smile remain forever. Of course, life wouldn't allow that. But as often as possible, Gabe was going to ensure that he made Tessa happy.

Gabe dipped his head. "I was surfing some online twin forums last night."

"Really?" Tessa grabbed a paper towel and gently dried her hands.

He shrugged. "My brain was a little too hyped up to sleep." In truth, the initial searches he'd done had nearly sent him spiraling. There was a reason that physicians always warned their patients not to go searching the web; you could find some truly terrifying statistics that would do nothing but worry you.

And there were more than enough medical horror stories about multiples pregnancy out there.

He'd finally found an identical twin forum and searched out funny stories to ease his tumbling brain. "I kept worrying that we might get them mixed up. Since, you know, identical!"

He made a silly face, enjoying the giggle that erupted from her. "Several parents recommended choosing a color or pattern for the little ones. One in yellow, the other in green. One twin in stripes and solids for the other bean. So you don't confuse who is who when they're newborns, though their individual personalities shine through pretty quickly, according to most of the parents."

Gabe had only meant to look at a few things, but he'd loved searching through the forums. Finding out new things about the next step he was taking. *With Tessa.*

It was easy to care about Tessa. Easy to be around her. Easy to fall in love—

No. That had not happened. But even as Gabe stared at Tessa's wrinkled palms, which were blessedly less red now, he knew that was wrong. He was already half in love with her.

Emotions swirled through him, a mixture of excitement, joy and fear as he looked at her. She was his second chance. What if he lost her?

His mouth was dry as that thought tossed around his brain. Losing the person he cared most about had nearly destroyed him before, and now it wasn't just Tessa he might lose.

No. He could protect Tessa and the twins. Make sure that nothing bad happened to them. Make sure that he didn't face the bottomless pit of despair he'd known when Olive passed. He could make sure everything was fine. And it would be easier as Tessa's—

Boyfriend was the wrong word. *Roommate*

made his skin crawl. The correct word refused to materialize. But Tessa's hand on his interrupted his mental wanderings.

"I said, I never even thought that I might not be able to tell them apart!" Tessa enunciated words that he'd missed while trying to work out ways to protect his family. At least she was unaware of all the thoughts racing through his mind.

"Sorry, I guess the day is longer than I thought." He stroked her palm, glad that twenty minutes under scorching water didn't seem to have injured her. "I read an article by a mom who swears she might have mixed her boys up on the day they came home from the hospital."

"That sounds like the hook of a bad sitcom— and all too possible!" Tessa's chuckle echoed in the small room. "We should definitely have a plan!"

Gabe wrapped an arm around her shoulder. "That's tomorrow's worry. Why don't I stop by Maggie's after my shift and meet you after you've talked to Patrick?"

She cocked her head, "Expecting it to go poorly?"

"No." Gabe was almost certain that was the truth. "Just looking for a reason to get some cupcakes."

"You don't need a reason, Gabe."

His heart burst as she winked and headed for

the door. "I cannot imagine a situation in which I would turn down a coffee cupcake. I may drink nothing but decaf right now, but I can at least enjoy that sweet treat!"

He offered another pretend salute and was rewarded with a brilliant grin before she exited. He'd bring her anything to make that smile appear. Seeing Tessa happy was the best part of his day. She and their children made him feel whole. It was as simple as that.

CHAPTER NINE

"I THINK IT'S time you got a new comforter for your bed!" Isla winked at Tessa as she followed Gabe up the stairs carrying a box of his belongings. "This one is not pretty. Maybe Tessa can help you pick another."

"It keeps me warm, Isla. It doesn't really have another purpose." Gabe took the lamp from Tessa's hands and kissed her cheek before setting it on his beat-up dresser.

Isla dumped what Tessa had to admit was an ugly comforter on the bed that Matt and Gabe had carried up an hour ago. "It's brown. And not a pretty warm coffee color. It looks more like…" Isla held her nose and smirked at her brother.

Tessa covered her lips to keep her grin from showing, but she caught Gabe's knowing look.

"This is the last one," Matt stated as he set another box on the bed. "And the comforter looks fine to me."

Gabe nodded to his brother before Matt headed

down the stairs again. The nonverbal sibling communication made Tessa's heart race. Gabe's family interacted with one another just like she'd always dreamed of. They were a family—a real family.

"Two against one." Gabe laughed as he hung up a stack of shirts.

"Nuh-uh!" Isla slipped her hand through Tessa's. "Back me up, Tessa!"

She felt her eyes widen as her gaze shifted between Gabe and Isla.

Crossing his arms, Gabe leaned against the wall. The smile he offered her sent desire spilling through her. Those dimples were a work of art.

"Do you think it's ugly?"

"No using the dimples." Isla stomped her foot. "He knows they have power."

Gabe threw his arms in the air. "Guilty."

Tessa laughed at the fun exchange. She hoped her kids would have this type of relationship. The love was clear between them, even as Isla judged her brother's bad taste in bedroom decor. This was the life she'd yearned for. The life her kids would get.

"All right." Isla nodded before facing Tessa. "Honest answers only, Tessa."

Biting her lip, Tessa glanced at Gabe and shook her head, "Isla's right. It is ugly."

Gabe flung a hand over his chest and playfully

threw his body against the wall. Tessa's and Isla's laughs echoed through the room.

"I guess the vote's tied then." Tessa shrugged.

"Oh, no, it's not. You count as three votes."

"Isla! My family would like me home for dinner. You coming?" Matt yelled from downstairs.

She offered Tessa a quick hug and high-fived her brother. "I'll find some suitable choices and email you, Tessa. The perks of being a department store buyer." She waved and disappeared.

"She never did play fair." Gabe laughed as he swung Tessa into his arms. "She means it, too. She'll send you a few choices and expect you to make me choose another comforter. Determined doesn't begin to describe Isla."

"They're wonderful." Tessa sighed before kissing Gabe's cheek. "Really, really wonderful." Tessa hadn't been sure how they'd react to Gabe moving in with her and becoming a dad, but the Davis clan had been nothing but loving.

"How about we get the bed cleared off so I can sleep in it tonight, then we can pop some popcorn and watch a movie? A nice night at home."

Tessa ran her hand along his chest. "That sounds lovely." And it did. Her heart swelled.

Such a simple word, with so much meaning. *Home.* Just replaying the sound of the word on his lips was enough to make Tessa's heart sing. Maybe this could work—truly work. Despite ex-

pecting twins and playing get-to-know-you—
really get-to-know-you—at the same time,
maybe everything would be all right. If she
hadn't been nearly in love with him already,
today would have sent her over the edge.

The words were on the tip of her tongue, but
their unorthodox start had already gone through
so many twists and turns. The last thing it needed
was her confessing that she was falling in love
with him the day he moved into her spare bedroom.

Telling him she loved him could wait. *But the
timing is perfect*, her heart whined as her brain
refused to operate her tongue. *Not today!*

Her phone buzzed, and she quickly glanced at
the text. Dr. Lin was asking if she could cover a
shift or three for him for the next few weeks. If
she said yes, she'd be at the hospital nearly every
day for a while. But if she said no—

No. That didn't seem like an option. In a few
months, she might not feel like adding extra
shifts.

Instead, she typed back a quick response and
then grabbed Gabe's hand. "We'll have to make
tonight count." She pressed her lips to his again.

"Oh?" Gabe wrapped his hand around her
waist.

She leaned into him, enjoying the feel of him,
the knowledge that he'd be here when she came

home. It calmed her. "Dr. Lin needs me to take a few of his shifts. I guess he's finally getting his retirement paperwork filed and starting some retirement courses that the hospital mandates its staff take before they out-process."

"How many shifts?"

Gabe's tone was light, but his gaze flickered with a touch of worry. The look disappeared behind a smile, but Tessa was certain she'd seen it.

"I'll be at the hospital most days. But it will give me another leg up when they fill his position. Plus, it means Patrick believed me when I said that my pregnancy wouldn't impact my work. I know he told a few of the staff and asked them to be discreet."

"But nothing is discreet among hospital staff." He kissed the top of her head before moving to grab a stack of pants from a box on the bed.

She couldn't control the giggle. "I think that may be one of the biggest understatements of all time. But I'm happy that my colleagues aren't treating me differently. At least for now, I can still take on extra shifts."

"I'm glad." He dropped the pants into a drawer. *Is he frowning?*

When he looked at her, Gabe's eyes were bright. He grabbed the few remaining boxes and set them next to the bed. "I can sleep in there now. Let's get our movie marathon going. I don't want to miss a single minute." He smiled again, but there was a flicker of something in his gaze.

Another uncertainty pushed through her. Was he upset that the hospital was still relying on her? Had he hoped she'd take a step back after they found out about the twins, even though he'd told her he'd support her?

"Rom-com or horror flick?" Gabe's grin chased away most of her worries.

But not all of them.

"Are those our only choices?" Tessa folded her arms.

"Nope. The choice is yours, my lady." He playfully bowed, and the final flutters of worry drifted to the back of her mind.

She was looking for ways to worry. Looking for reasons her world might implode. Just because it always had did not mean this was destined for failure. She was going to have a family—a real family.

After weeks of extra shifts, Tessa was reaching levels of exhaustion she hadn't experienced since she was a resident. It must be the pregnancy, because she'd kept long hours since she'd started at Dallas Children's. Often it had been easier to be at work than at home.

Following her divorce, she'd increased her hours even more. Anything to avoid the daily reminder that she had a job she loved but an empty house. A few days of double shifts were normal for her, but today, she was dragging.

Her stomach let out a growl as she started for the cafeteria. The granola bars she'd always kept in her pocket for between-meal snacks at work didn't come close to satisfying her. In fact, most days, she felt like she could eat her way through an entire grocery store and not burst!

"You look like you could use a strawberry smoothie." Gabe's voice was bright as he held up the cup. "Complete with a meal replacement supplement for hardworking doctors."

"You don't need to spoil me." She cocked her head and playfully folded her arms across her chest.

"So, you don't want it?" He smiled as he held the smoothie.

"Of course I do!" She grinned as her belly let out a growl loud enough for Gabe to hear.

"What would you do without me?" Gabe winked and took a big sip of his smoothie.

The smoothie stuck to the back of Tessa's throat. His tone was playful. He was kidding with her. There wasn't an underlying unhappiness. It didn't mean anything.

He leaned as close as was professionally responsible, and her heart jumped. "I also put a few snacks in the employee fridge for when I'm off in a few hours."

"Thank you." Tessa squeezed his hand quickly before dropping it. Gabe had made sure that she had a packed meal and several snacks to get her through the shifts. He'd been great and so reliable.

Too reliable. Tessa hated that niggling thought. Over the last week, he'd taken on so much at home. More than she'd ever expected.

It would be easy to rely on Gabe—to let him handle so many things. But hadn't that driven Max away?

Why wouldn't that thought disappear?

No, her heart screamed. Tessa could let Gabe handle little things. That's what partners did. They shared the load—without complaining.

Besides, if everything fell apart, she was more than capable of remembering to pack snacks. But what about protecting her heart?

"We've got a burn victim en route!" Fran, a triage nurse, called.

Tessa took another giant swallow of her smoothie before dropping it on the nurses' station. Gabe had made sure that her name was written in bold letters on both sides. Even if it was melted, it would provide the calories she and the twins needed. The man thought of everything.

His smoothie dropped beside hers, too, and they quickly made their way to the ER bay doors. Burns were common in the summer and fall. Children touched hot grills and burned themselves roasting marshmallows, but those emergencies usually resulted in a frantic parent bringing their child in. If an ambulance had been dispatched...

Her chest was tight. The waiting was the worst. Knowing that a seriously injured or ill child was incoming and needed support sent your adrenaline into overdrive. But the wait made your body doubt the reserves it was pouring forth. Tessa rocked on her heels and felt Gabe's strong body right behind her. He didn't touch her; he was prepping for the arrival, too. But just knowing he was there calmed the electricity racing along her skin. They made an excellent team—and could handle whatever was coming through the door now.

"Amy fell next to a pit where her family was roasting a pig. Caught herself with her hands in the coals," the paramedic called as he pulled the doors open. "Parents were distracted with a work call and left her in charge. Amy is eight."

Gabe heard the collective gasp of the staff that was waiting. It was impossible to work in a children's emergency room and not see unfit parents. Far too many individuals prioritized things that could be replaced over their children, which could not.

His mother's choices hadn't resulted in any of her kids taking a trip in an ambulance. But only because Gabe had become hypervigilant watching his younger siblings. If he'd been younger or less responsible, things could have been much worse when their father hadn't been around to act the way a parent was supposed to.

Anger, tension and a hint of fear raced along his spine. How could anyone do anything other than treasure their family? Prioritize anything over their children?

He forced his emotions into lockdown as the paramedics pulled the gurney down and passed the paperwork to the waiting admitting nurse. Being mad at her parents wouldn't help Amy. Hopefully, this would be a wake-up call for them.

"Hi, Amy. I'm Dr. Garcia, but you can call me Tessa. And this is Nurse Gabe. We're going to make sure you're all right." Tessa offered the child a smile, but her knuckles were white as she gripped Amy's gurney.

They treated so many things that resulted from accidents. Things that couldn't be helped. Kids flipped on their bikes and skateboards, trampoline injuries, but it was infuriating when it was the result of neglect.

"I didn't mean to mess up." Her whimper was so soft, and it broke Gabe's heart. "My hands hurt."

Tessa ran a hand along Amy's forehead. "This is *not* your fault."

He watched Tessa shake a bit of the fury away before she met Amy's gaze. "We're going to give you some medication to make it feel better."

Gabe saw Tessa swallow as they turned into the room. Burn patients were a medical professional's worst nightmare. The risks of infection and loss of use of an appendage were much higher than with other wounds. Plus, patients had a tendency toward shock within the first twenty-four hours of injury.

But it was a good sign that Amy's hands hurt. It meant that the nerves were still intact. Unfortunately, it also meant that she would deal with a significant amount of pain while she healed.

"Pain management first, then initial debridement," Tessa stated as she put the orders into the computer tablet before turning to check the child's wounds.

The paramedics had loosely dressed her hands. When Tessa removed the dressings, Gabe saw her cheeks twitch. Second-degree burns covered both her palms and most of her fingers.

Amy sniffled. The child had to be in significant pain, but she was doing her best to hide it.

Gabe got down on her level. Maybe no one paid much attention to her at home, but here she was their primary focus. "What's your favorite color?" Tessa was going to need to clean the wounds, and even with the pain meds she'd ordered, it was going to hurt. Distracting Amy was the best thing he could do for her right now.

Where are the child's parents?

"Purple." Amy's voice was wobbly but strong. She wasn't in shock—at least not yet.

Denise entered with the pain meds Tessa had ordered and quickly administered them to Amy. The child didn't even flinch as Denise placed the needle into the meaty part of her arm.

"You're very brave." Gabe smiled. "Not many adults can just get a shot and not flinch. I cried the last time I got one."

Amy's eyes narrowed, but she offered him a tiny smile. "Really?"

"Cross my heart!" Gabe grinned. "I was hiking and fell on some rocks. I got a big cut on my leg that got infected. They gave me an antibiotic called Rocephin. It hurt bad."

"But you're okay now?" Amy's words were quiet, but he could hear the real question behind them.

His throat was tight, but he forced out, "Yep. Even the scar is less noticeable now. And *you* are going to be okay, too."

Amy's eyes teared up as she nodded.

As she exited the room, Denise looked over her shoulder. "Your mom is here. She'll be in as soon as she finishes her phone call."

"My parents are always on the phone."

The resignation in the little one's statement cut across him. The few times he'd visited his mom after the divorce, she'd always been on the phone, too. At least he'd had his dad to make sure he knew that he was important. But it hurt to know that something else mattered more than you. It was a cut that might heal, but the scar on your heart never disappeared.

His children would never believe that anything was more important than them. They wouldn't have to beg for attention like he had from his mom. Never wonder if he loved him.

"Gabe's right. You're going to be okay, but we have to make sure your hands are clean." Tessa smiled at Amy, but Gabe saw the subtle twitch in her hand. This was going to hurt, even as the pain meds took effect.

Amy swallowed and looked at Gabe. "You'll stay."

"You bet." Gabe patted the top of her head. "I'm here for you." He knew those words would comfort Amy, but he also glanced at Tessa. He was here for her, too—whatever she needed.

* * *

Gabe started from his bed. His brain thought he'd heard something, but the town house was silent. He rolled his head from side to side a few times, straining to hear any sound.

Nothing. He blinked and rolled over to look at his clock. He'd tried waiting up for Tessa. After taking care of Amy's burns, he'd thought she might need someone to talk to. Particularly since she'd been vibrating with anger as she talked to the child's parents, who'd seemed more concerned with their jewelry shipments than their daughter being admitted to the burn unit.

He'd waited after his shift ended, but Tessa had needed to handle one of her additional duties as the senior attending. He hoped she found the Thai food in the fridge and his good-night message.

It had been their routine since she'd started taking on additional shifts. The quick kisses as he passed her in the morning and the occasional stolen time for a smoothie at the hospital were so unsatisfying. At least she only had two more days of these nightmare long shifts before she rotated back to her regular schedule.

Was this really the position she wanted? And how much time would it steal from their family?

Gabe glared at his ceiling and threw an arm over his eyes. This wasn't Dr. Lin's shift. It was his and most of Tessa's shifts combined. She was working all the hours she could legally muster to prove herself to Human Resources, for a position that they hadn't even sent out an official announcement for.

What would their lives be like when the actual competition started? Gabe had watched doctors contend for positions before. He knew how cutthroat the healing professions could be when positions that rarely opened were competed for. It would have been daunting anytime—but she was pregnant. *With twins.*

"So, what else can I do to help?" The walls gave no answer to his whispered question as he tried to calm his mind enough to drift back to sleep. He was off tomorrow. At least he could make sure Tessa had a solid meal before she headed back to the hospital.

Assuming she'd even come home. She'd slept in the employee suite a few nights ago and quipped about it reminding her of her residency days. Gabe had nodded as she talked about it, hating the circles under her eyes and worrying about her increasing focus on the hospital. He was doing his best not to voice his worry that she was operating on too little sleep for a physician and a pregnant woman. Tessa knew her limits.

But would she listen to them?

"Argh!"

The scream echoed down the hall from Tessa's room. Gabe's feet hit the floor.

He didn't stop until he was next to her bed.

"Gabe?" Tessa's eyes were open, but her voice was dreamy. He wasn't sure she was really awake. She couldn't have been home for long, and asleep for even less time. She had to be exhausted.

"I'm here." He sat on the bed and stroked her hair as she lay back down.

"I dreamed there was an accident." Her hands flew to her belly, and she sighed. "Dream..." Her voice was soft as she shifted her head on the pillow.

He dropped a kiss along her temple. "Pregnancy hormones can make dreams more vivid." Stacy had talked about how crazy her dreams had gotten after her first trimester. From birthing cats to her brain pulling the most horrific things from her subconscious.

Tessa's subconscious had more than enough material to make her dreams grim. Especially following a nightmare scenario at the hospital, and the fact that she was already running herself into the ground.

He stroked her back. She looked so beautiful in the moonlight as it streamed through the window. *And exhausted.*

When her breaths became even, he dropped another kiss to her temple and stood. They both had Monday off. And Tessa was going to do nothing but be pampered. She deserved to be taken care of for at least twenty-four hours.

He'd make sure they had plenty of popcorn for an epic movie marathon.

"Gabe?"

Would he ever tire of hearing her say his name? He hoped not. "I'm still here," he whispered.

"Stay with me." She pulled the covers to the side and slid over. "I don't want to be alone. Please."

The quiet plea nearly undid him. He joined her in bed and pulled her close. "I'm here." He kissed her shoulder as he wrapped his arm around her waist. She fit snuggling against him, and his heart soared as she sighed and slid back to sleep.

He tried to stay awake a few minutes to make sure that she was all right, but his eyelids kept drifting closed. Soon he gave up and let himself drift away, too.

Tessa rolled over and smiled as she stared at Gabe's lips. He'd come running last night. She couldn't remember the dream that had woken her so soon after she dropped into bed. But she could remember asking him to join her in bed. And how safe she'd felt as he slid his arms around her. How safe she felt lying in his arms now.

She ran a hand along his jaw, enjoying the

feel of the bit of stubble under her fingers. They hadn't seen much of each other outside the hospital lately, and she was surprised by how much she hated that. It had been normal for her to basically live at the hospital before she met Gabe.

The employee suite, where staff routinely caught a few extra hours of sleep, was a regular overnight stay for Tessa. Gabe had looked so shocked when she'd slept there on Wednesday that she'd made up a story about it reminding her of her residency days—which it technically did—but also it wasn't uncommon for her.

But last night, she'd driven home rather than stay. Even if they weren't sharing a bed, she wanted to wake up in the same place as Gabe. Wanted to have breakfast with him.

And she'd asked Dr. Killon to cover the final two shifts for Dr. Lin. She wanted the senior attending position, but she was too tired. It wasn't safe for her patients or for the twins for Tessa to be so exhausted.

For the first time in years, she had three days off in a row. And Tessa planned to spend as much of it as possible in Gabe's arms. She dropped light kisses along his jaw, slowly working her way toward his lips.

He stirred as her lips met his. "Good morning." Gabe managed to get the words out between kisses.

"I missed you." Tessa ran her hand along his back, enjoying the feel of his skin beneath her fingers. She doubted there was a better place to wake than in Gabe Davis's arms.

"We live together, you know." Gabe's fingers traced up her thigh as he kissed her nose. "But I missed you, too. It would be nice to share more than just a few passing kisses and smoothies." His lips pressed against hers as he shifted his hips.

Tessa pulled him back. She wanted him— all of him—this morning. She let her lips trail along his shoulder as her fingers wandered farther south, and she enjoyed the hitch in Gabe's breath as they edged ever lower. "That isn't exactly what I meant." Tessa slipped a finger along the edge of his boxers.

Gabe gripped her hand, stilling its advance. "There is nothing I want more. Promise." He sucked in a deep breath. "But the next time I make love to you, I want to take my time."

He nodded toward her nightstand. "Your alarm should go off any second. I'm a little surprised it hasn't already."

"Dr. Killon is taking Dr. Lin's shifts for me today and tomorrow." Tessa pulled his face to her and kissed him—deeply. His hands trailed along her back, creating tiny bolts of electricity with each light stroke. "I have the next three days off."

Before Gabe could fully react, Tessa rolled him onto his back and started trailing her lips down his body.

In the morning light, he was stunning. And he was hers. That sent such a rush through her as she listened to his breathing increase.

Gabe's hands wrapped through her hair as she worked her mouth lower. When she slipped his briefs down, Tessa grinned.

She'd been wrong. There *was* a better way to wake up than in Gabe's arms.

CHAPTER TEN

"You have to be gentle with the seeds." Tessa pulled his hands out of the pot she'd handed him and gently rearranged the seeds he'd pushed into the soil before tossing dirt on top of them. Then she patted the soil and set the small pot to the side.

Gabe watched the process for the fourth time. He kissed her cheek as she laid another small pot in front of him and handed him more seeds. "I hate to break it to you, sweetheart, but that was *exactly* what I was doing."

Tessa's light chuckle made happiness burst through him as she stepped into his arms. Her hands wrapped around his neck before she kissed him. "I am patting the dirt, Gabe. You were mashing it."

He really didn't see the difference, but he'd stand next to Tessa all day while she worked with seeds. She'd decided last week that they should have a winter garden. Tessa was intent on trying the small garden ideas she'd found in the books she'd been leaving all over their living room. It would be nice to have fresh veggies, though Gabe believed she might have more fun growing the plants than anything else.

The bedroom he'd briefly called his own was now a veritable greenhouse. Grow lights were set up on a few small tables with labels announcing each pot's seeds and the watering schedule that needed to be handled for each grouping. This made Tessa happy, and that made Gabe happy.

Happy. Gabe stared at Tessa as she darted between her pots. His heart sighed at the image as he drank it in.

Life had dealt him an unimaginable loss. He'd never expected to feel this again. To relish the simple days at home. To be part of a family outside of the one he'd been raised in.

It was a gift. One he planned to hold on to tightly. To protect.

He'd do anything for Tessa and the twins. Anything to earn a permanent place next to her. *Forever.*

She planted another kiss on his cheek as she stepped beside him. Then her brow furrowed. "I got dirt on your chin." She held up her hands, staring at the dirt splatted on them. "And I've no way to wipe it off."

"You've had dirt on you since we stepped in here. It hasn't stopped me from wanting to kiss you yet." He shrugged. "What's a little dirt when you—" Gabe managed to pull back, barely.

Clearing his throat, he gestured to all the seeds. "When you're having such a good time."

Blood pounded in Gabe's ears as her beautiful brown eyes stared at him. The words *when you love someone* had nearly slipped into the space between them. His heart screamed for him to finish the statement. To declare what he wanted to believe was between them.

The last few weeks of living together, working together, watching her belly expand together had been some of Gabe's life's happiest. The hole in his chest that had refused to seal when he lost Olive had closed more the closer he got to Tessa.

He'd always miss Olive. But finding love again was a precious gift. And he was going to protect his family as much as possible.

"I was thinking about the nursery." Gabe pushed the seeds into the pot, barely controlling his grin as Tessa monitored his motions. When she accepted his pot and set it with the other spinach plants, Gabe thought his heart might shoot from his chest. *Success!*

"I know you wanted to wait a little while longer." He accepted another pack of seeds and a pot as Tessa started watering the plants on the far table. "But I think it's pretty obvious what theme we should go with."

"Theme?" Tessa raised an eyebrow as she looked over her shoulder at him. "I wasn't aware that we were actually going to have a theme. Is that a little overboard?"

Tessa's hands rested on her belly, and he knew that her shirt was going to have a dirt stain just over where their children were growing. It only cemented his idea. Gabe gestured to the seed pods around them. "Gardening! Picture it." He squeezed her shoulder tightly. "A room with images of flowers, green blankets, maybe even a few of their mother's plants in the corner."

He pulled the loose plan he'd sketched from his back pocket. "See."

Her dark eyes misted over as she ran a finger over the paper. "You did all this?"

"Of course. I love doing things for you and the babies. As much as you enjoy dirt and seed pods." He kissed the tip of her nose—one of the few spots that was dirt-free.

"That is a lot! Because I do love dirt and seeds." She giggled as she looked at her fingers. "I think cartoon characters and woodland creatures are more standard."

He shook his head as he pointed to the sketch he'd made. "Standard is boring. Besides, I think we should lean into the twin parent thing. Two peas in a pod and all." He kissed the top of her head.

Touching Tessa, being with her, watching the small bump where the twins—his twins—were blooming, was exciting. He'd go all out at being a twin dad. Double strollers, minivan and all.

Tessa pulled one lip to the side as she looked at him. "I like this, but we have to make one change." She put a finger against the dirt, then added another thimbleful of water on the plant. "What if we find someone to paint a snowy mountain hiking path into a garden? A combination of us. And that is as close to a hiking trail we will be—at least until the twins are older."

Gabe hadn't realized it was possible for his heart to expand more. But his chest bloomed as she pointed to where the mural would be on the paper. "That would make this design perfect."

Tessa's grin lit up the room. "I never expected you to be so involved in the entire process. Max hated any decorating. I was all prepared to have to pick out all the colors and furniture on my own." She rocked back on her heels as she stared at him. "You are amazing. I lo—" Her eyes darted to the pots as she folded her arms. "I love the fact that you are so invested in our little family."

His ears burned as he stared at her. It felt like there was more to that statement. Or at least he wanted to believe there was. But Gabe didn't want to push—at least not yet.

Handing her another pot, he smiled. "I enjoy picking stuff out. Helping you, researching car seat standards, safety regulations—protecting our family in the cutest way possible." Gabe winked. "Besides, I'd do anything for our kids." *And you.*

Tessa started toward him and then abruptly stopped. "Oh!"

It took him three steps to reach her, but Gabe's heart felt like it was dropping from his chest. "What's wrong? Do I need to call the doctor? Or Emergen—?"

She grabbed his hand and placed it on her abdomen. "The babies are moving." Her smile was bright as she laughed. "Oh, it feels so funny! Like dancing gas. Wow. Not the cutest description I could have chosen. Though accurate."

His skin felt clammy as the adrenaline leaked from his body, and his stomach twisted. There was no danger here. *Nothing to worry about.* "You scared me." He hadn't meant to say that, and he saw compassion and concern float in Tessa's eyes.

Her fingers were soft as they touched his cheek. "You can't jump to the worst case." Tessa leaned her head against his chest. "I know you lost Olive, but you couldn't have known that she had an aneurysm. And Dr. Fillery said just two days ago that at seventeen weeks along, I am healthy, and the babies are doing great. Breathe with me."

Pulling in a few deep breaths, Gabe tried to remind his heart to slow. It was still too early for him to feel the twins twirling around her belly, but Gabe didn't remove his hand from Tessa. The connection grounded him.

His leap to calling the emergency line was too much for a light comment. But when you'd lost everything once, the urge to protect what you could engulfed you.

Letting the worries float away, Gabe enjoyed the feel of Tessa pressed against him. The feeling of rightness that echoed through him in these small moments. The movies made grand gestures seem like the epitome of romance. But they weren't.

It was these simple moments, with a hand on the belly where your children were growing, surrounded by spinach, lettuce and winter squash seeds, that made the best memories. "Sorry. I just…" He shrugged as the words and worries refused to materialize.

Her lips were warm as they pressed against his cheek. "I understand." Tessa trailed her fingers along his jawline. "We're fine. Promise."

He dropped a light kiss along her lips, sighing

as she deepened it. "I also know you'll refuse to let me wrap you in Bubble Wrap for the rest of your pregnancy!"

"Nope. No Bubble Wrap. Too much to get done!" She held up a tiny pot containing a winter squash and marked the bottom.

She was always on the go. They'd yet to have another movie marathon or spend more than a few minutes relaxing on the couch since his first night here. The woman seemed incapable of slowing down.

"What are you thinking for dinner?"

"Oh!" Tessa held up her hand before reaching in her back pocket. "That 'oh' was because my butt was vibrating." She held up her phone. "Finally!"

Gabe playfully put his hands over his ears as her shout echoed in the room. "I'm scared to ask." Though he suspected only one thing would have sent such an excited yell through the small room. The job was finally open. The thing she wanted so badly.

He swallowed the touch of panic clawing at his throat. *It will be fine.*

Tessa danced like she had all those weeks ago before holding the phone to his face.

Gabe tried to put on a cheerful smile as he read the confirmation of what he already knew. "So, Dr. Lin's position is open."

"Yep!" Her voice was an octave higher than normal. "I'll probably put in for a few extra shifts here and there. Pad my application and all." She smiled.

More shifts. Did she really have to take on more work? Spend more time away? Wasn't her expertise enough to speak on its own?

He bit back an objection as Tessa's eyes roamed his. He cared about her, loved her. He wouldn't dampen this moment with his own fears.

"I'll pace myself. Promise."

Gabe pulled her to him and rested his head on hers. "I'll do anything I can to make this easier." Tessa wanted this position, and he wanted her to succeed. He did.

His throat closed as he tried to stop the flutter of worry arching its way through his belly.

"Anything and anytime, right?" Tessa kissed the tip of his nose.

"Right," Gabe responded, hating the tingle in the back of his skull. There was nothing wrong with wanting a promotion, with wanting to reach for everything. *Nothing.*

Tessa wasn't his mother. She'd protect herself and the twins. All these fears were the past. If only he could get his heart to listen to his mind. Stop the bead of worry that lit up in his chest any time Tessa talked about the promotion.

She wasn't going to choose work over her family. She wasn't. Besides, Gabe was going to be the best partner he could be. He'd make sure she was as comfortable as possible at home.

If he did everything for her, she'd realize that being home with him and the twins was just as exciting as being at the hospital.

Tessa had never felt as exhausted and achy by the long shifts as she had over the last week. Just walking the floor was enough to make her yawn.

Growing children is hard work.

Her stomach grumbled again, and she popped a few blueberries that Gabe had packed into her mouth. Then she playfully glared at her expanding belly. "I am literally feeding you now!"

Or so it seemed. She smiled as she rubbed her belly.

Tessa had begun showing. She was enjoying each of these new steps. Though with as much as she was at the hospital, it felt like she was in danger of letting it fly by.

Stroking her belly, she grabbed another mouthful of berries. The selection process for the senior attending should be completed before Tessa hit her third trimester. She could dial it back a little then.

Or you could withdraw your name from consideration.

Her stomach lurched as the idea tossed around

her brain. It was just the fatigue talking. She'd given up one senior attending position. She wasn't walking away from another.

The twins...

Tess quashed that thought before her exhausted brain could finish it. Her mother had lost her career because of an unplanned pregnancy. Tessa wasn't relinquishing this chance because her path to motherhood had been unexpected.

She was just tired. That was all.

The twins moved, and Tessa's nerves quieted a little. During her third trimester, she was sure she'd be uncomfortable as they danced and battled for the ever-decreasing space in her abdomen. But for now, it was the best feeling ever!

Hopefully, Gabe would feel it soon. She planned to memorize every moment of that event. He was going to light up, with that big grin that made his eyes nearly disappear. She loved that smile. Loved how much he'd taken on without her even asking.

Being protected by Gabe was a blessing she'd never counted on. He'd made life so much easier. She'd missed being taken care of.

Though a tiny kernel of worry still hid in the recesses of her mind. She never wanted Gabe to resent all his help. For him to wish that she hadn't taken advantage of the job opening. But it was easy to ignore the tiny voice when he held her in arms.

Her buzzer went off, and Tessa grabbed a final handful of blueberries before heading for the nurses' station.

"We've got twin boys in room four. One needs stitches in his arm and cheek. The other has an ankle the size of a baseball. Triage ordered an X-ray." Debra passed over the tablet chart.

Tessa looked over the triage report. A pair of seven-year-old boys had jumped out of a tree house.

"The mother is beside herself. Just so you know."

"I bet." Tessa tapped the chart. Children never calculated dangers into their adventures. She knew her own two were likely to send her into a panic many times before they hit their teens. And then a whole new host of worries would likely begin.

"Daddy!"

The stereo echo hit Tessa as she closed the door and turned to greet her patients. Identical pairs of watery eyes hit her, and her heart exploded as her own future stared back at her.

Offering a smile, Tessa stepped toward the table where the boys were huddled together. "Nope. I'm Dr. Garcia."

"I want Dad," the one that had a large gash on his right arm stated, before glaring at his mother.

"Dad will be here when he can. But I'm here, DeMarcus." The woman's dark gaze met Tessa's. "We're separated. He always handled everything. Never complained—" She caught a soft sob and forced a tight smile. "Collin said he'd be here soon."

Tessa nodded. She'd seen all sorts of family dynamics during her medical career. "It's all right. Can you tell me what happened?"

"We tried to fly," the little one with an ice pack on his ankle offered.

"And crashed," DeMarcus finished.

"But next time—"

"There will be no next time, Dameon." Their mother's lips pursed as the statement echoed off the walls. "Sorry."

The door opened and a tall man with the boys' curly hair stepped into the room.

Both the boys' eyes lit up.

"I thought I heard you, Eva."

The twins' mom shook her head and gestured toward the boys. "They're already plotting how to jump off the tree house again."

"Without crashing," Dameon added.

Both parents sent a look toward their son, dutifully ignoring looking at each other.

"We are going to X-ray Dameon's ankle."

Tessa raised her voice, trying to regain some control of the room. The tension between the boys' parents vibrated, and she saw the twins squeeze each other's hands. It was always difficult when marriages ended, but when children were involved, the stakes changed.

She'd dealt with many struggling parents and all sorts of custody issues as a physician, but the focus had to be on the boys right now. "And DeMarcus is going to need stitches in his arm and cheek."

"Guess it's a good thing I remembered the insurance card and snacks." Collin's words were clipped as he passed a bag to his wife. "You need to do some of these things, Eva."

"I'm trying." Her words were tight as she looked from Collin to her boys. "There's just so much."

"Which I've always done."

Tessa crossed her arms as she stared at the warring pair. This was not helpful. "Why don't you two take this conversation to the hall while I start DeMarcus's stitches." Tessa smiled, hoping the oncoming quarrel could occur away from the boys.

The radiology tech stepped into the room and moved aside as Collin and Eva took their argument to the hallway. "Who am I taking for a ride to the X-ray machine?"

"Me!" Dameon shouted, but when he moved, the color drained from his young face.

"Careful, little guy. Let's get some pictures of that ankle." He nodded to Tessa as he took the child out.

"Let's see if we can't get you stitched up." Tessa smiled as DeMarcus stared at the closed door.

"I miss Daddy living at home."

The sadness in his childish voice caused a lump at the back of her throat. There was nothing she could say. His parents weren't divorced—yet—but it hadn't sounded promising.

"You might feel me pulling on your arm, but if you feel any pain, let me know and we'll make sure we give you some more numbing." Tessa hoped her smile was comforting, but DeMarcus's gaze never left the door.

"Dad makes better mac and cheese than Mommy. But he was tired of doing everything while she was at work. They yelled a lot. But I miss the mac and cheese."

"I bet," Tessa conceded. Children missed a lot less than their parents thought. "You're a very brave little boy."

The door opened again, and Collin stepped through. "Sorry, Doctor."

Tessa nodded. She wouldn't say that arguing

in front of your kids while they were waiting on stitches and X-rays was fine.

"Are you coming home?" The wistfulness in DeMarcus's voice hung in the room as his dad's shoulders slumped.

"I love you, buddy. And I love Mommy, too." He choked back a small sob. "But...not right now."

"He needs to keep these clean and dry for the next two weeks. After that, the stitches should be fully dissolved. One of the nurses will give you information on infection. And once we have X-rays back, we'll see what we need to do for Dameon."

He nodded. He still wore his wedding ring. Maybe their marriage wasn't completely over.

You need to do some of these things.

His words sent a shiver through Tessa as she left the room. She was still independent. Wasn't she? Sure, she liked Gabe taking care of her. She'd let him take over so much while she took on extra shifts. He hadn't complained, but Collin hadn't, either. And neither had Max at first.

Her lunch rolled in her stomach as Tessa tried to think of anything she'd contributed to the household over the last few weeks. Her mind produced very little. She'd ceded so much to him...

Was she setting herself up for another disaster?

Her phone buzzed, and she felt her frown deepen as she stared at Gabe's words.

Oil changed! And I got the grocery shopping done. Don't worry, I didn't touch the plants. How about we do takeout? I'm exhausted.

She'd told him she'd take the car to the mechanic this weekend. And she'd planned to do the grocery shopping on her way home. Though after a long shift, could she really be upset about this?

She bit her lip as the realization struck her. Tessa was independent—she was. But hearing the twins' parents' argument highlighted how much she'd changed over the last few weeks. She'd been relying on Gabe. For *everything*.

That would not do. She didn't want her twins to live DeMarcus and Dameon's reality. Hadn't she learned from her marriage that people didn't always mean it when they said they didn't mind? She loved Gabe. She never wanted to see him exhausted because she hadn't pulled her weight.

She could make a few changes. Ensure that Gabe didn't resent her like Max had.

"Ouch!"

Gabe started toward Tessa as she put her soapy finger to her lips. "That can't taste very good."

He reached over and turned off the water, trying to control the frustration in his belly. He'd told her he'd clean up, but she'd insisted that she do the dishes since he'd cooked.

It was one of the many things she'd asserted control over this past week. The more he tried to assist at home, the more she insisted that she didn't need it. How was he supposed to help, to show how much he cared for her? No matter how he tried to lighten her load, she seemed intent on doing more than her share.

And she brushed off all his offers of help. That stung. He was happy to do things for her. Happy to make sure that she was taken care of. She'd told him the night they'd reconnected that no one had protected her—cared for her. He was here to do that.

If she'd only let him.

"I'll admit that a mouthful of soap is not appealing. But when I broke my nail, it was just an automatic reaction." Tessa looked down at her fingers. "That's the second one I've broken today. Guess I need to pay better attention, huh?"

"Second one today? Do you think your iron levels are okay?" Dr. Fillery had warned them that moms of multiples often ended up with vitamin deficiencies that weren't serious if they were caught early. Tessa had put the list of symptoms on the fridge, even though as a doctor she knew them. Just as a reminder.

Gabe passed her a glass of lemonade. "This should cut the taste of soap."

"You have a bank of knowledge on the taste of soap?" Tessa smiled before taking a few deep swallows.

"It was one of my mom's favorite punishments for saying curse words. I only got the punishment once, but Isla received it several times." Gabe frowned as he glanced at the list of low iron symptoms. Tessa had several. But it could just be that she was working so much.

His brain wrapped around the worries as he tried to shake himself. History was not going to repeat itself.

"Why don't I finish the dishes?" Gabe sighed as she held up the last dish.

"All done!" She yawned again and looked at her watch. "Can we postpone movie night? I'll just fall asleep in your lap."

He'd be fine with that. Gabe would never tire of holding her, but it was probably better if they went straight to bed. Leaning over, he kissed her cheek. "Of course." This was at least the sixth movie night they'd tabled.

His gaze drifted to the list once again before he focused on the woman in front of him. He was worried about her and the twins. Sucking in a deep breath, Gabe raised his concern. "I know you've been tired lately, and brittle nails can be a sign of low iron. Maybe we should talk to Dr. Fillery at your next appointment." He nodded toward the sheet on the fridge, hoping she'd understand.

"No, we don't need to raise this with Dr. Fillery." Tessa pushed a hand through her curly hair before stepping into his arms. "Deep breaths, Gabe. This isn't a medical crisis. I am working more right now and growing not one, but two babies. A little tiredness is to be expected."

Except this didn't feel like a little tiredness. She yawned several times an hour, despite regular naps and falling asleep as soon as her head hit the pillow. "And the nails?"

Tessa sighed before she met his gaze. "I broke two nails, Gabe. Relax. Please." She squeezed his hand. "I'm fine. This is just what happens when you fail to keep your nails trimmed. The prenatal vitamins are making my nails grow faster than normal."

Her hand rested on his chest, and she grinned. "There isn't anything wrong with me, Gabe. Other than your two children are sucking up all my energy."

"What about cutting back at the hospital?" Gabe knew they were the wrong words as soon as they left his lips. But there was no way to reel them in—and this was a conversation they needed to have. He knew she wanted Dr. Lin's position, and Tessa wasn't the only physician doing their best to prove themselves indispensable to the hospital.

And Dallas Children's was more than happy to take on their extra labor. It was a script he'd seen play out several times throughout his career. A hospital exploiting a cutthroat competition to get the most out of its workforce was standard. He'd participated in it at his hospital in Maine, too.

But a job was not worth hurting yourself or your family for.

"That's not an option, Gabe." Her hands slapped the counter before she crossed her arms. She was preparing for battle.

He didn't want to fight, but he was concerned. "It is," Gabe countered. Tessa was exhausted, and if her record and résumé didn't stand on its own, did she really want the position? "You are not required to burn yourself out for Dallas Children's. Doing everything is not possible."

He watched her take a deep breath and tension seeped from her shoulders. Tessa sighed. "I appreciate the concern." She stepped beside him. "I really do." Her lips were cool as they pressed against his cheek. "I'm a physician. I know all the signs for low iron and a multitude of other ailments. I'm fine. I promise. I don't need you to protect me."

The words cut as he held her gaze. There was so little he could do right now. She'd started packing her own lunches and insisted on dividing the chores equally. She got upset if he did something that she'd declared was her job. Protecting his family and those he loved brought him the most joy. Helping was how he showed his love.

But if the woman he loved didn't want his help...

His sister's text ringtone echoed in the kitchen, and Gabe was grateful for the interruption. He needed a few minutes to gather his thoughts.

Barbecue Saturday. Three o'clock. You bring the chips and salsa.

"Everything okay?"

No. But Gabe didn't want to discuss the divide that he felt was opening between them. Tessa was stressed enough as it was. Part of Gabe was worried that she'd tell him she didn't need him at all if he pushed her to take it easier. And he wasn't sure he'd survive that.

"Stacy is having a barbecue Saturday. I know you're working the evening shift on Friday."

"But my Saturday is still free. Unless Dr. Lin or someone needs..." Tessa shook her head. "No.

I am free, and I won't pick up another shift then. I promise."

She was choosing family time. Choosing *him*. The ball of tension in Gabe's chest relaxed a little on those words. It refused to dissipate completely, but at least it was easier to breathe. For now.

"I'm going to hold you to that. And I need to raid the cilantro plant—we are supposed to bring chips and salsa."

Tessa kissed his cheek, and more of his worry slid away. "I'll cut some. Just tell me how much you need."

Before she could walk away, Gabe pulled her into his arms. Her shoulders were tight, but they relaxed as he kissed the top of her head. A tiny thump got his attention, and he pulled back. "Was that…?"

Tessa's brilliant smile warmed his heart as she put his hands on her belly. "Yes!" She placed her hands on either side of his cheeks. Her face was bright with happiness as her gaze roamed him. "I promised myself that I'd memorize every moment of you feeling the twins for the first time."

"You did?" Gabe laughed as a foot or elbow pushed at the hand he had on her belly.

"I knew it was a memory I would never want to forget." Joyful tears hovered in her eyes. "And

I was so right. I can't wait to watch you be a dad."

She released her hold and laid her hands over his as the twins twisted in her belly.

His children…*their children.* Tears coated his eyes as Tessa leaned her head against his shoulder. Most of his final worries slid away as she let out a soft sigh, and their children kicked his hands.

CHAPTER ELEVEN

"HOW ARE YOU DOING?" Isla handed Tessa a glass of punch.

Gabe was playing with his nieces and nephews on the lawn. He lifted a little girl high in the air, spinning around fast before collapsing with the child on the lawn. Peals of laughter rang across the patio.

Warmth and happiness bloomed in her chest. Tessa was watching a snapshot of the future—her future. Their children would never feel like they had lost their family. No matter what happened in their lives, they'd have a place here.

"I'm doing okay." It was the truth, mostly. She was tired, but that was the normal state for her now. No matter how many naps she took, she couldn't shake the exhaustion. But nothing was going to keep her from enjoying every moment today.

She loved watching Gabe with his family. He was going to be such a good father. And she was going to make sure that he never felt taken advantage of. *Ever.*

Her free hand rested on her belly as she took in the fun scene and sipped her punch.

"You know it's okay if you aren't." Isla laughed as a nephew jumped on Gabe's back and screamed for him to be a horsey.

Tessa barely controlled the yawn that pulled at the back of her throat. She'd gotten eight solid hours of sleep last night and even taken a nap in the car on the ride over. There was no reason for her to be so tired. *Maybe you should talk to Dr. Fillery.*

"The Davis family can be a lot." Isla raised her glass to Stacy's husband as he carried their screaming toddler inside. "I swear I've lost a few girlfriends because I introduced them to my family. One didn't even make it to dinner before telling me that we had a nuthouse."

She wrapped an arm around Isla's shoulder and squeezed. "Your family *is* a lot. A lot of fun and love."

They cringed as a toddler, whose name Tessa hadn't learned, squealed. The sound echoed into the woods behind Stacy's house, and a group of birds took flight.

"And a lot of noise, too." Tessa winked at Isla. "Anyone who can't see the happiness here, and run toward it, isn't worthy."

This is what Tessa had always dreamed family was. The rowdy, joyful nature thrilled her. Her mother had done the best she could, but she couldn't magic a room of cousins for her to play with. No fun weekends with aunts or uncles. She sighed as she soaked it up.

Isla smiled as she raised her drink. "You're perfect for him. Even if you let him keep that ugly brown comforter."

Tessa laughed as Isla's pronouncement sent a thrill through her. Her eyes misted, and she ran a hand across them. *Hormones.*

The noisy Davis family was wonderful. And her children would be so loved here. With cousins galore!

"Thank you. I know this has been a different path." As the statement escaped her lips, Tessa wished she could withdraw it. Those words may have been right a few weeks ago—but they didn't feel accurate now. What did it matter how she and Gabe had gotten here?

"Your brother is special. He makes me happy." Those words brought another round of mist to Tessa's eyes. Second trimester waterworks were definitely stronger than first trimester ones. Her eyes might be constantly wet by the third trimester if this trend held.

"Yes." Isla leaned close. "Gabe is special, and

you make him happy. I wasn't sure that was possible after—" Her voice died away.

"After Olive passed," Tessa finished for her. "You can say her name. It doesn't bother me. Gabe will always love her. I know that. But his heart is big enough for both of us."

Isla wiped a tear away from her cheek. "I'm so glad you're part of our family, Tessa. And you, too, little ones." She laid a hand on Tessa's lower belly. "Two more little girls!"

Tessa giggled. "I am delighted to be an honorary family member. But we decided not to find out what sex the babies are. Better to be surprised. Though I am wavering on that decision now."

Gabe had said it was her decision, and she'd wanted to be surprised. But she also wanted to know if Gabe was going to have two little girls to dote on or two boys they'd have to keep from trying to fly from tree houses. Though she'd patched up lots of little girls, too… They were going to be busy—and happy.

Isla shrugged as she looked back toward Gabe. "The twins are girls. I've guessed every one of my nieces and nephews correctly. Those are feisty little girls—*trust me*. And Tessa." Isla waited until she looked at her before continuing. "You aren't an honorary member of anything. The Davis clan is your family, too."

Her throat closed as she met Gabe's youngest sister's gaze. Isla really meant it. Before she could say anything, the babies twisted in her stomach, and suddenly she needed to find the restroom. "Thank you, Isla. You have no idea how much that means. But I need to find the bathroom. I think the twins have started playing hockey with my bladder!"

"Ahh, the joys of pregnancy!" Isla cooed. "At least, so they tell me." She winked again and quickly gave Tessa directions.

"I swear, you two need to find a better toy." Tessa joked while washing her hands. She knew that carrying twins meant even less space for the two of them to move around, but at twenty weeks along, she felt like she was constantly feeling them argue over who got to kick her kidneys.

She stepped into the hallway and yawned. This was out of control. She was *not* tired! At least not enough to yawn every thirty seconds.

"Isla has claimed Tessa as her new best friend. I think she plans to spoil your little ones to pieces. And she swears the twins are girls." The voice of Gabe's oldest sister, Stacy, was light as it traveled from the other room.

"Well, she's been right every other time." Gabe's laugh sent a small thrill through Tessa as she laid a hand over her stomach. If there were two girls in her belly, he'd be the perfect girl dad. But Tessa wasn't ready to buy girl dad stuff based on Isla's predictions.

"I don't care. As long as the twins and Tessa are healthy."

Tessa's heart expanded as the twins danced around her belly. Gabe had told her he didn't care what they were having, but hearing it repeated to his family was nice too. How had she gotten so lucky?

"I'm glad you found Tessa. She's perfect for you."

Tessa smiled. She really was part of the family. *Family.*

"She is. I just wish she'd relax some." Before Tessa could announce her presence, Gabe continued, "I'm worried about her getting this promotion."

Tessa's chest clenched and it felt like cold water was splashing across her dreams. *What?*

"Brett, stop practicing karate takedowns on your sister! I swear that girl needs constant attention." Dishes clinked, and Tessa heard Stacy turn the sink off. "I thought you said Tessa was really qualified."

She wasn't sure she wanted Gabe's explanation; eavesdropping wasn't a trait she wished to cultivate, but her feet refused to move. Maybe he was worried she'd be disappointed if the hospital hired someone else. Maybe it wasn't about Tessa getting the promotion.

Maybe this wasn't a repeat of Max. Gabe had said he was happy. Except he'd talked about her pulling back the other day. And he'd hesitated to date her because of the job.

Her brain rattled with worries as she twisted her palms together. *Please.*

"She's very qualified. That's the problem. If she gets it, well, I worry what that means for our family." His voice drifted away.

The happiness bubble in her chest burst. That Gabe could question her ability to be present for her family cut a deep wound across her heart.

Did he think her getting the promotion would make her less of a mother? She didn't want to answer that question. Tessa wasn't sure her heart was strong enough to handle it.

Squaring her shoulders, she rubbed away a tear before she stepped into the room. "Is there anything I can help with?" She hoped her smile looked real, even though it felt so false.

Gabe's gaze shot toward her. His jaw clenched, but he didn't ask if she'd overheard the conversation.

"Yes." Stacy smiled as she handed her a plate of cookies. "Can you put these out—but tell the kids they only get one!"

"Of course." Tessa's voice felt odd, and she

couldn't quite bring herself to meet Gabe's gaze. Even as she felt it rake across her. If she looked back, Tessa feared she'd force him to explain his worry about the promotion now. This was not a conversation she wanted to have with an audience.

It wasn't a conversation she wanted to have at all. She loved him. Tessa was almost positive he loved her, too. But if her advancing at Dallas Children's was a problem—

She'd never live with someone who looked at her like Max had. She couldn't do that again.

"Oh, and we're doing ladies' night in two weeks. Friday night tacos while the boys watch the kids. It's not a late night anymore, just a few hours away from the madness. You should come." Stacy's smile made Tessa want to weep.

She wanted to go. Desperately. Wanted to belong to the Davis family. Fully. But this place would always be Gabe's. Their children would belong here, too. But if she got the promotion, and he left her…

Tessa barely controlled the sob clogging her throat. Her soul ached at the idea that she might not be welcome here someday. The Davis family felt like…like family. Her family.

Her heart screamed for her to say yes. To take the risk, to trust that Gabe hadn't really meant that it would be a problem if she got the job. But she would not make the mistake she'd made with Max's friends. If Gabe wasn't sure what would happen if Tessa got the promotion, she couldn't let herself get too close to them. No matter how much she might want to. "I have to work."

"The schedules aren't out yet," Gabe stated.

His eyes held a look that she couldn't quite read. But she already had a ready excuse.

"I promised Dr. Lin that I'd work a few final shifts with him." It was mostly the truth. Dr. Lin had asked, but she'd told him she had to think about it.

She saw Gabe's lips turn down, and her heart seized. How was she supposed to ask him about this? Until Tessa could find the right words, she was just going to pretend everything was fine. At least with the extra shifts, it would give her an excuse for putting it off.

Tessa smiled, and she caught Stacy's gaze. "Thank you for the invitation. It means a lot." *More than you could know.* She bit back that final statement as she lifted the plate of cookies.

Stacy smiled. "Don't let the kids talk you into more than one cookie. They are cute but diabolical!"

"I won't. Cross my heart." Tessa nodded to Stacy before she let her gaze drift to the man she loved. They'd never said that they loved each other, but her heart was his—completely. But if Gabe didn't feel the same way…

She forced those thoughts away. Now was not the right time or place. And the last thing she wanted to do was break down in front of Gabe's entire family. No, there'd be plenty of time to figure out what Gabe meant—and what it meant for their future.

"Cookies!" Her call was choked, but the kids came running. And Tessa let some of her fear go. Even if she wasn't destined to be part of this clan, at least her children would always have a place to call their own.

The sheets next to him were cold as he rolled over. Tessa hadn't come home—again. That made two nights in a row that she'd slept at Dallas Children's. Two nights she'd chosen an uncomfortable hospital sleeping room over their bed.

He flopped over and stared at the ceiling. His heart hammered as he tried to push at the doubt pooling in his belly. Something was wrong.

Tessa was putting distance between them, but Gabe didn't know how to draw her back. How to fix the situation. How he could help more when she seemed intent on proving that she didn't need it. Didn't want it.

Or maybe she was just too busy trying to ensure she got the promotion to notice the gulf between them. Maybe the promotion was more important than sleeping next to the man who loved her. His mother had felt that way.

Gabe pushed his palms into his eyes, willing the horrid thought away. But his brain refused to choose another track. What if this promotion wasn't enough? What if he wasn't?

He loved Tessa. Wanted to be with her. But waking up alone to cold sheets was not something he'd settle for. Being an afterthought to a parent left scars that never completely healed. He didn't want that for their children—or for himself.

He blew out a breath as he swung his feet from the bed. The few times he'd seen her this week had all been when they were on shifts together. There was no way to have a discussion during that time. No time to address whatever was bothering her.

And how could he help if he didn't know why she was avoiding him?

He started the coffeepot, adding an extra scoop of grounds. He needed as much caffeine as the pot could create. Pulling open the fridge door, his heart squeezed as he looked at the meal he'd packed for Tessa. It was still sitting on the top shelf. It was ridiculous to get upset about a packed lunch. Particularly since he was sure she hadn't been home.

Maybe she didn't *need* his help, but why didn't she want it? It was a gesture of love; couldn't she see that? Didn't she want his love?

The garage door opened, and Gabe rubbed his palms on his blue jeans. She was home, and they needed to talk. But his fingers twitched as the worry ricocheted through him. What if he didn't want the answers?

So many thoughts and emotions chased through him. Ambushing Tessa as soon as she got home from the hospital wasn't ideal. But when else was he going to see her?

"You're awake." Her gaze hovered on the coffee cup in his hand.

The dark circles under her eyes were even deeper now than they'd been three days ago. *Is she okay?*

"I'm glad you're home." Gabe started toward her, but she barely paused long enough to let him kiss her cheek before she pulled open a cabinet and grabbed a granola bar and coffee mug. Gabe tried and failed to stop the pain that caused. When was the last time they'd kissed—really kissed, not just a peck on the cheek?

"That's not decaf," Gabe stated as Tessa poured the coffee and put a lid on it.

"It's okay." She sighed as she took a deep sip and ripped open the granola bar.

Having up to two hundred milligrams of caffeine a day was fine during pregnancy. But Tessa had refused to drink anything but decaf since finding out she was pregnant. He bit back his list of questions about her health and chose what he hoped was a safer topic.

"Rough night at the hospital?" He sipped his own drink as he slid next to her.

"Yes. Two car accidents and a trampoline injury that resulted in compound fractures of both tibias." She let out a sigh and took another sip of coffee before pouring the rest of it down the sink. "As much as I want to suck this down, I probably need a few hours of sleep first."

Yes! Gabe smiled and set his coffee mug next to hers. "Do you want me to tuck you in?"

Her gaze shifted as she stared at him. "I am working every day but Friday next week."

Her chin rose, and Gabe felt the air in the kitchen shift. There was a script—he was sure of it—but he didn't know which words she expected him to say. "I'm not sure what that has to do with my questions, but okay. Maybe after next week, you could take a day or two off."

"Why?" Her voice was tight, and there was a fire in her eyes that sent a shiver down his back. She was exhausted, and there had to be a better time to discuss this. But he wasn't sure when the opportunity would show itself. "Because you will have been living at Dallas Children's for the better part of two weeks by the time those shifts are over."

"The other physicians are doing the same," Tessa countered, and straightened her shoulders. "Josh Killon has a newborn and two other little ones at home, and he is working similar hours."

"Working hours like that only proves that Josh Killon doesn't care about his wife or family. The man cares only about himself." Gabe wanted to kick himself as the words flew between them. That wasn't what he'd meant to say—though it was the truth.

Tessa looked like he'd slapped her. Gabe bit the inside of his cheek as he shook his head. "I know you aren't like Josh."

"Do you?" Tessa's eyes twitched as she met his gaze.

No. Yes. That had been an unfair statement. Even if Tessa was spending more time at the hospital than home, even if he hadn't seen her in two days, she didn't see people as stepping stones like Dr. Killon did.

If he could have pulled his words back, he'd do it. Swallowing, he took a step toward her. "Yes. Dr. Killon only cares about himself."

He took a deep breath and pulled on all his

reserves. He shouldn't have compared her to Dr. Killon, but there was a topic they needed to discuss. "But you should understand better than most that working to exhaustion is a recipe for disaster."

Tessa's eyes narrowed. "Meaning?"

"You have dark circles under your eyes. You're exhausted. What if you had fallen asleep on the drive home? Your mom was working so hard that she fell asleep behind the wheel."

Damn it! He hadn't meant to say that, either. *Why is your brain refusing to provide better words?*

"Sorry, Tessa. I'm messing all of this up."

"You're wrong."

The cool tone of her voice sent a wave of panic down Gabe's back.

Her eyes were clear, and her shoulders were firm as she met his gaze. "My mother didn't die because she was working too hard. She died because she left med school to have me. She died because my father got tired of supporting everyone and abandoned us."

Tessa hiccuped as she wrapped her arms tightly around herself.

"But would she have wanted you to push yourself to the edge for a job? A promotion isn't more important than family. It isn't worth injuring yourself or the babies." Gabe pushed his hands through his hair as he caught the final words.

Tessa's eyes widened and the final bit of color slipped from her face. "Do you want me to get this promotion, Gabe? Or are you hoping that Josh Killon or Mark Jackson gets it?"

"No one wants Josh to get it." The joke fell flat as Tessa raised an eyebrow and tapped her foot.

Swallowing the fear, Gabe shrugged. "I want so many things, Tessa. I want to protect you and the twins. I want to provide for you. I want you." He tried to say he wanted her to get the promotion. Those were the words she wanted to hear— but they refused to materialize.

She was exhausted. She looked sick. No job was worth that. Why couldn't she understand that?

"I'm here for you. Let me carry some of the load." The plea fell from his lips. *Please.*

Tessa's eyes flashed with tears, but they didn't spill down her cheeks. "We can share the load, but I don't *want* you to do everything. I don't *need* you."

Gabe blinked as her words pummeled him. "I see." Helping others, protecting them, was what Gabe did. All the things he offered to do for her, she didn't want him to do. Didn't need *him.*

At least not like he needed her. That was a painful truth. His heart cracked as he stood next to her. The walls felt like they were closing in as he tried to push back the hurt. What was his role if he couldn't help the woman he loved?

"I need to get some sleep, but Patrick talked to me today. I have an interview for Dr. Lin's position next week." Tessa walked past him. "I thought you should know.

"And I heard you say at Stacy's barbecue that you were worried I'd get the position." Her voice cracked. "I can do this, Gabe."

Her shoulders slumped as she stood in the doorway. The final bit of fight draining from her. "I will be a great senior attending."

She would. Gabe offered a small smile. "I'm sure you will. But Tessa, you can't do it all." *At least not alone. And you don't have to.* But his tongue refused to say the words his heart cried out.

Pulling at the back of his neck, Gabe tried to find a path forward, anything that let him be in her life as more than just the father of their children.

How had the dream shattered so quickly? He'd watched his mother pull away from her family for years. Watched her put a little more distance between her and their father. Gabe wouldn't wait around to watch history repeat itself.

"Maybe I should stay at Stacy's for a little while." The words fell into the space between them. The obstacles this conversation had highlighted radiated around them.

Her bottom lip shook, and Gabe swallowed. If she asked him to stay, he would. He would do almost anything for the woman in front of him. *Just ask me to stay.*

"If you think that's best." Then she turned and left.

A hole opened in his chest as he stared at the empty doorway. How were they supposed to cross this chasm? The clock ticked away, and his heart cracked with each step he climbed.

Tessa was already fast asleep. She hadn't even pulled the covers down on the bed. Gabe grabbed a bag and threw in as many of his clothes as he could. Then he grabbed a blanket and pulled it over her.

Running his hand along her temple, Gabe didn't try to stop the tears falling down his cheeks. "I love you." At least he'd gotten to say the words once. Then he turned and fled the place he'd hoped would be his forever home.

CHAPTER TWELVE

TESSA WATCHED GABE walk to his car from the shadows of Dallas Children's parking garage. Her heart screamed for her to run to him. To yell for him to come home. To plead that three lonely nights was more than she could take.

To tell him she loved him and see if that could right the chasms between them.

She'd given up one career opportunity for a partner. And he'd left her anyway.

But Tessa hadn't expected Gabe to leave. That was the part that pummeled her. She'd been exhausted and had needed a nap to regroup. To find better words to explain.

When she'd woken she'd smiled at the blanket he'd thrown over her. She'd gone to find him, hoping to work through the divide that had opened between them. To apologize for her harsh words.

But his things had been gone. His bed was still in the room where they'd first put it. Still covered with plants. But his clothes were gone. The pictures of his family had been taken from the fridge.

When he'd offered to go to his sister's, she'd assumed it was only for a night. Just to give them each a day to cool off.

Not for good.

She hadn't even spoken to him in three days. Three long days of silence. She'd drafted and discarded so many text messages in the last seventy-two hours. Tessa grabbed her phone and pulled up Gabe's number. *Again.* She'd never realized how difficult it was to press Send.

She yawned and slid her phone back into the pocket of her scrubs. Even if she'd known what to say—what the proper apology was—she didn't have time right now.

Closing her eyes, she sighed. She'd been at the hospital nearly every day this month. Even before he'd left, she'd packed her lunches, handled her share of the household chores—made sure that she was carrying her part of the load. And it still hadn't kept Gabe in her life.

It had driven him away.

What if Gabe really had enjoyed taking on so much? Enjoyed picking up extra chores so she could rest? Truly enjoyed helping her, instead of resenting her? What if she'd been so concerned with the past that she'd ruined her future?

His crushed face hovered in her memory. Her words had done that. She'd told him she didn't need him. *Didn't need him.*

That was the biggest falsehood she'd ever spoken. She needed Gabe more than she'd ever needed anyone. Not to help her around the house, but to love her. To believe in her—and that terrified her. Instead of clinging to that amazing gift, she'd let fear rule. And lost everything.

Her chest clenched as she started for the hospital entrance. Tessa put her hand to her heart as she tried to catch her breath. Spots dotted her vision as she tried to force her feet to move faster, but it felt like she was wading through quicksand.

Her skin was clammy, and panic raced across her spine. This wasn't a symptom of the broken-hearted. Her hand reached for her belly as she crossed Dallas Children's threshold.

"Dr. Garcia?" Denise's voice was far away.

"I…need…an ambulance." Tessa's chest clenched as she tried sucking in air. Blackness pulled at the edges of her vision, and she tried to keep it away.

Gabe… She tried to say his name. *Maybe she had.* But as the darkness took her, Tessa wasn't sure she'd managed to get it out. *Gabe…*

Dr. Fillery offered a nod as she walked into Tessa's room at Presbyterian Hospital. She didn't remember being transported here, but Tessa didn't care about how she'd landed here. She had only one concern.

"The babies."

"Are fine. My concern is about you." She strode to the bed. "Your iron levels were dangerously low, Tessa."

Dr. Fillery's voice carried an authority that she recognized. It was the *I am a doctor and I need you to follow the orders I am about to give* voice. Tessa had used it many times in her career.

She didn't care what Dr. Fillery said she needed to do. The twins were fine. She let out a soft sigh as she let that knowledge wrap around her. The babies were okay. A kick to her ribs sent a smile to her lips. Tessa rested her hand over where the twins were wrestling.

"You're staying here at least overnight, Tessa. You will need to take an iron supplement for the rest of your pregnancy and likely through at least the first few months postpartum." Dr. Fillery took a deep breath and then offered the final order. "And you need to take at least the next two weeks off at Dallas Children's. I know your patients are important, but your hemoglobin levels were at four point two grams per deciliter. I can't believe you were still standing."

"I'll take time off." She meant it. Tessa wouldn't fight the orders, but the forced time off carried other consequences. She bit her lips as the tears coated her eyes. It was fine. *It was fine.*

"If we can't get your levels regulated, I'll recommend bed rest. But right now, I'm just going to tell you to stay home, rest as much as possible, eat lots of leafy greens and lentils. I'll see you in my office at the end of next week, and we'll see if you're strong enough to go back to work then."

Tessa nodded, but the blood was pounding in her ears.

She'd have to cancel her interview—pull her name from consideration. She'd worked so hard for the senior attending position. She was the most qualified. It hurt to step away from it. But Tessa wouldn't risk the health of her children—or herself.

Still, she let a few tears fall for the lost opportunity. There'd be other job openings, she knew that. But that didn't fully chase away the pain.

Her throat was tight, but she pulled up her phone. It wouldn't take long for the gossip network at Dallas Children's to rehash one of their doctors collapsing as they started their shift. She didn't want Gabe to worry.

Besides, he deserved to know that their children were all right. She typed a few words, then hit Send. Then she gave in to the exhaustion chasing her.

* * *

"Brett didn't eat all her lunch today. Do you think she's feeling all right?" Gabe put the cheese stick and uneaten grapes back in Stacy's fridge.

His sister's scoff echoed in her kitchen as she passed him a plate and a towel. "She's almost thirteen, Gabe. Lunchtime is more about socializing than it is about eating lunch. Besides, she told you that she only wants tuna and carrots. I know you're bored, but let the preteen pack her own lunch."

The statement sent a pain down his back. The fissure over not speaking to Tessa for the last three days was bursting at the seams. But he took a deep breath and forced the feelings back inside. He wasn't going to break down—at least not right at this moment.

It was a constant battle to just pretend to be normal when everything seemed lost. Colors no longer seemed as bright, and food—even the sugary treats he loved—had no flavor. Without Tessa, the world was bland.

Leaning against the counter, he tried to shake off the despair that had clung to him since he'd walked out of Tessa's town house. *Keep moving forward*; it was the mantra he'd used after Olive passed. The one that had eventually broken him. But Gabe wasn't going to let that happen—not again.

Besides, Tessa was still alive. Still at Dallas Children's. Still pregnant with their children. Still so many things—but not his.

He needed to get control of himself. "I'm just trying to earn my keep. Brett's barely been home between school, martial arts and dance. I swear that kid is always gone!"

The excuses fell from his lips as the truth ate through him. Tessa hadn't wanted his help, hadn't needed it. He was trying to ignore the hole their argument had torn through him. Who was he if he couldn't help the people he loved? If the woman he loved didn't want his help?

Stacy raised an eyebrow before dipping her hands into the soapy water again. "Help is appreciated, but Brett needs to do things for herself—it builds character."

"Mom! We're going to be late to weapons class." Brett's voice was high-pitched as she raced toward the garage.

"No running in the house!" Stacy dried her hands before putting her hand on his shoulder. "And Gabe—" his sister's smile was tinged with an emotion he feared was pity "—you don't have to do everything for everyone. There's no need to earn your keep with family."

Gabe didn't move as his sister grabbed her purse and rushed to the car. Crossing his arms, Gabe stared out the window of the back porch.

Memories of Tessa laughing with his family played out before him, and pain raced through him.

There's no need to earn your keep.

His sister's words ate through his soul. He wasn't trying to. Not really.

Except...

He squeezed his eyes shut as the truth settled within him. After his mother's abandonment, Gabe had taken on more responsibilities. To help his dad and make sure everyone was cared for. To be enough...

Enough that a job wouldn't be worth more than him.

Tears blurred his vision when he opened his eyes. He'd tried for years to be "enough," so his mom would come home. To be more important than the career she'd given everything up for. But Gabe would never be enough for her—no one would.

But that wasn't because there was something wrong with him.

A weight he hadn't known he was carrying lifted off his chest. He was enough—just as he was.

But now he had to address how he'd let that fear destroy his family.

Rather than tell Tessa he loved her, he'd tried to earn his place in Tessa's life. Tried to be more important than her promotion. Because he was worried that she'd choose that over him. Like his mother had.

And she had.

The specter of hurt raced across his heart. But the truth cried out, too. She'd said they could carry the load. *Together.* That she didn't need him to do everything. She'd wanted a true partnership. And he'd wanted more. To be the protector who rode to the rescue.

She'd asked for a partner, and he'd walked away because she wasn't looking for a knight in shining armor.

The woman he loved had asked if he wanted her to get the thing she'd worked hard for. A job that she would excel at, and that would enable her to help others. She had a passion for serving others that their children would see and learn from. A true partner would have screamed, *Yes!* But he'd walked away—because he'd feared that one day she might choose it over him. Because leaving felt safer than getting left.

But Tessa was not his mother. He'd lost love once. But this time he'd thrown it away on the minuscule chance that he might get hurt.

How was he supposed to fix this? He banged his head against the kitchen cupboards, trying to force some idea to present itself. This couldn't be fixed with cupcakes or some other treat. He needed some grand gesture—something to prove...

No!

Gabe was done trying to prove that he was enough. But he needed to figure out a way to show Tessa how much he loved her. How lost he was without her. How much he wanted to stand beside her as she achieved her dreams. *All of them.*

His phone buzzed. His hands were clammy as he ripped the smartphone from his back pocket. He still wasn't sure of the right words, but he didn't care. He needed her.

Always.

The twins are fine. I don't know if you heard, but I passed out at the start of my shift. I will be at Presbyterian overnight. Then two weeks of strict rest. I'm going to pull my name from consideration for the job. You were right. I can't do it all.

The words devastated him. She was brokenhearted over the job—and he'd contributed to that. He'd made her feel that she couldn't do it all. He could have tried to be more understanding. Tried to see her asserting her need to help him as wanting to be his partner.

Instead of seeing that as a blessing, he'd given in to his own anxiety. And he'd shown her that she might have to rely on herself in a world without him. Gabe slapped the top of his head. *God, he was a fool.*

But Gabe could fix part of this. He made a quick call, then grabbed his keys. There was one errand to run, and then he was going to see Tessa. He was going to apologize, to confess his love, and to promise he'd stand by her no matter what.

Presbyterian Hospital didn't have bright walls or pretty murals to ease the hospital feel like Dallas Children's did. As Gabe raced toward Tessa's room, his chest tightened. It had taken him almost two hours to get everything together.

A nurse brushed his shoulder, and his backpack shifted. He'd grabbed the items he'd thought might make her stay more comfortable. He didn't pause to make sure the one breakable thing was fine. If he had to buy another because her mouthwash leaked, Gabe would. He would not waste any more time getting to her side.

Her door was closed. Gabe took a deep breath to keep from rushing through. If Tessa was resting, he didn't want to wake her.

Only the small lamp was lit, but she turned as soon as he walked through the door. Her tentative grin sent a flash of hope through him.

Even after everything that had happened, she'd reached out to him.

His heart leaped. He'd never walk away from her again. *Never.*

"You came."

Her whispered words cut across him. Gabe hated that she had doubted for even a second that he'd come to her. He never wanted her to worry about that again.

"I will always come. No matter what. Because I love you." The words fell from Gabe's lips as he slid in next to her bed. "I know there are a million other things that I need to say, apologies to make, but I need you to know that I love you, Tessa Garcia. All of you."

Her fingers wrapped through his, and tears coated her dark eyes.

Before she could say anything, Gabe rushed on. "I was trying to earn your love." He brushed his lips against her hand as the words rushed out. "All the chores, the dinners, the cupcakes—I needed to prove that I was worthy. But I never meant to make you feel like I didn't believe in you. Like I didn't think you could do it all, or that I wouldn't want to walk beside you from here to eternity. I am so sorry."

"Oh, Gabe." Tessa turned in the bed as much as the rails would allow. "You never need to earn my love. My whole heart is yours."

He thought his body might erupt from happiness as she held his gaze. "I love you." He would never tire of saying those words.

Tessa bit her lip and squeezed his hand. "I was so concerned about making sure that you didn't feel like I was taking advantage of you that I pushed you away. Max may have hated when I leaned on him, but that was a fault in him, not me. I love you, Gabe Davis. What if we just promise to look forward now? Let the past stay where it belongs."

"That's the easiest promise I will ever make. I can't wait to spend each day with you, Tessa." Gabe ran his hand along her arm, unable to keep from touching her.

She wiped away a tear and gestured toward the room. "This isn't the best setting for a happily-ever-after, is it?"

The sterile room wasn't the location that he'd have chosen for this moment, either. Outside of their twins' birth, Gabe would be happy if he never had another night sitting next to Tessa in a hospital bed. But there was a bit he could do to brighten her room.

"I know you won't be here for more than a day or two—"

"One day, I hope." Tessa rubbed her belly as she interrupted him. "Though I'll stay as long as I have to."

How could he ever have doubted the woman he loved would choose anything over her family? If Gabe could kick his past self, he would. He knew the lifetime he planned to spend with Tessa was going to have valleys, but he was going to do everything in his power to make her happy every single day.

"I thought this might make it easier to stay overnight." Gabe pulled a small succulent from the front pocket of his backpack. "This was the smallest guy I could find—and you said they were hardy, so I figured a ride to the hospital wouldn't cause it too much worry."

Tessa grinned at the small plant. "You brought a plant. That's great. And it brightens the room."

"That isn't all I brought." Gabe took a deep breath and pulled out the router. He understood her raised eyebrow as she stared at the box. "It will make the internet at the house super strong. No dropped streaming videos."

"Oh." She nodded. "That will be helpful while I'm stuck at home. Lots of shows to catch up on. And movie marathons to enjoy."

"I can't wait for a movie marathon. I'm going to pop so much popcorn!" Gabe squeezed her hand and waited for her to meet his gaze before he continued, "Want some company in there?"

He sighed as she scooted over in the large maternity bed. When she curled into his chest,

Gabe's world finally felt like it was nearly right. But it wouldn't be complete until Tessa had the chance to chase her dream. "But this isn't for movie marathons. At least, not completely. It's so there's no chance of your video freezing during your interview next week."

"Gabe." Her voice wobbled, but she sucked in a deep breath. "I'm not interviewing for the position."

"Why not?" He ran a hand along her side. "You're the best candidate, Tessa. Everyone knows it. I should have said it three days ago. I should have told you how great a senior attending I know you'll be. I should have encouraged you to get a little rest, but I should never have made you doubt yourself." He kissed her cheek as her lip trembled.

"I appreciate those kind words. I really do. And I'm not giving up on the dream. But there will be other positions. You and the twins come first. Always." She smiled, but he could see the hint of sadness still hovering in her eyes.

"Don't get mad." Gabe kissed the top of her head. "But I called Patrick before I went to get that router. There's no reason you can't do a video interview. They're even interviewing at least one outside hire that way."

"An outside hire!"

There was the fire he loved so much. "Yep. If

you really want to pull your name from consideration, I will support you, whatever you want, but make sure it's because that's what you want, not because a crazy terrible week made you think you can't do it. Because you can."

"If I get the job, you'll have to take on more at home with the twins." Tessa looked at the router. "It won't be even."

The words were music to his ears. "No one's keeping score, Tessa. I promise."

"But I'll always handle the plants."

"Absolutely." Gabe ran a finger along her cheek and then bent his lips to hers.

The kiss was sweet and long. It spoke of all their hopes for the future. The years of love and happiness that spun out before them. *Together.*

EPILOGUE

"I'M HOME."

Gabe's deep voice echoed down the hallway, and Tessa smiled.

She would never tire of hearing him say that he was at home. However, today she was trying to surprise him. And she wasn't quite ready!

"Hold on!"

Tessa pulled the cake from the bakery box. It had flowers all over it—and Maggie's had promised that this green icing wouldn't leave stains on anyone's teeth. The sugary scent floated up as she set it in the middle of the small dining table, and one of the twins kicked.

Whoosh! At nearly thirty-two weeks along, they were almost out of room in her abdomen, but they still managed to level at least a few good jabs every day. But Tessa really didn't mind.

"Behave!" She glared playfully at her belly. "Or I might let Daddy eat all the cake."

Another rib shot.

"Tessa? Are you all right?"

"Fine," she called. Adjusting the silverware, she let her gaze wander to the decorations she hadn't had time to lay. *Oh, well.*

Swinging open the door, Tessa bowed as much as her belly would let her. "Dinner is served."

Gabe raised an eyebrow before dropping a kiss to her cheek. "This looks lovely. And that cake is making my mouth water. What's the occasion?"

She knocked his hip with hers as they walked to the table. "You pamper me. All the time!" After she'd taken over the role of senior attending, Tessa and Gabe had slipped into a routine that worked well, but he deserved some indulging, too.

"And you love it." Gabe's lips were soft as they brushed against hers.

Yes. She did.

"True." Tessa smiled. "But you deserve a night off, too. I'd have put up more decorations, but the delivery guy was running late."

"Decorations?"

She bit her lip as she gestured toward the cake. "Isla is driving me nuts with all the girl stuff. Figured we might want to know so we can get serious about choosing names! What better way than dinner and a gender-reveal cake."

The bristles on his cheek sent waves of need racing across her as Gabe pulled her close and kissed her. She leaned into him. Hope, excitement and love pulsed around them. And then the twins kicked.

"They're getting strong!" Gabe laughed.

"I know!" Tessa tapped his side as she gathered herself. "Do you want dinner or dessert first?"

"Like you even need to ask." Gabe ran a finger along her chin. His eyes held so much love that Tessa felt like she might take flight. "Cut the cake and tell me what we're having."

She quickly slid the knife through the frosting and smiled. *Pink.* "Isla's winning streak holds true. Girls!"

Turning, she barely managed to set the piece of cake on the table. Gabe was down on one knee. His smile was so big as he held the ring out to her.

"I love you so much."

"Yes!" Tessa yelled.

He shook his head, and a small chuckle escaped his lips. "I didn't even ask yet." He pulled the ring from the box and slid it on her finger.

"I love you." Tessa smiled at the ring, and then at him. "But if I don't feed your little girls, I think they might start rearranging my ribs."

He pulled her close as the twins kicked. "Definitely a dessert-before-dinner night!" He bent and kissed her belly. "But don't get used to it, girls."

* * * * *

If you enjoyed this story, check out these other great reads from Juliette Hyland

A Stolen Kiss with the Midwife
Falling Again for the Single Dad
Unlocking the Ex-Army Doc's Heart

All available now!